TURNS OUT I'M AN EVIL ALIEN EMPEROR

LOU TRELEAVEN

To Chris, my co-adventurer

on Earth and beyond

1

TURNS OUT SOMEONE'S UP TO THEIR OLD TRICKS AGAIN

I'm Jasper, and last month I found out I was an alien. I also found out that my real parents are slugs and that I'm the rightful heir to a planet full of green slime.

This month, things have got *really* weird.

For instance...

I'm sitting behind a giant desk, the size of a double bed, in a huge glass-walled office that appears to be floating in space. That's just an illusion: it's not floating at all. In fact, it's at the top of a very, very high building, so high it pierces the cloud layer of AndroSphere (that's the planet I'm on) and thrusts into the black depths of space itself, giving me a stunning view of the mighty and almost invincible Andromedan Galaxy.

Sitting on the desk in front of me is a large holographic manual. I can see scenes from the reign of Iko Iko Iko, Son of Iko Iko, Grandson of Iko, Emperor of Andromeda Galaxy and Lots of Other Places Too playing out in front of my eyes in glorious 3D.

I've seen enough. I know what to do.

I press a button on the desk.

"Yes, Your Awesomeness?" a subservient voice squeaks through a little speaker.

"Send her in, Clerk Ninety-Nine."

"Yes, Your Magnificence."

"Oh, and bring me a chocolate milkshake. I'm thirsty and hungry at the same time."

"A... a what?"

The worst thing about being on a different planet is that the simple things just aren't simple anymore. "A chocolate milkshake. With a straw."

The voice shakes. "But... Clerk Ninety-Nine

does not know what a toklat mikeshike is, Your Gloriousness."

"Find one!" I bellow at the speaker. "And stop referring to yourself in the third person!"

"Clerk Ninety-Nine is sorry, Your Wowzerfulness. I mean, I am sorry, and I will. Try to find you a dockdock mookshook I mean—"

"A chocolate milkshake, you idiot!" I stand up and thump my tail. Yes, I have a tail. We'll get to this.

The 3D holographic manual jolts and opens up at the page showing Emperor Iko Iko Iko meeting the peace ambassador from Alpha Centauri. He is also standing up and thumping the table. The Emperor I mean, not the peace ambassador who is floating in a calming bubble with its legs crossed and a blissful smile on its face.

The door slides open with a *beeeeeep*.

"Oil that door or I'll have whoever is responsible killed!" I growl. From somewhere far down the corridor I hear a shriek and a thud, as the person responsible faints with fear. "Well, come in, if you insist," I say.

"General Shootemdown reporting for duty, Your Forcefulness, sir."

I sigh and consider thumping the table again. Why does no one know what to call me? I should standardise my title. But so much to do. You would never guess I have over a thousand staff. Most of them are too scared to talk to me and hide whenever I'm in a one hundred metre radius. Some are bolder.

I glare at the nasty little lifeform in front of me, whose arms have been genetically reengineered into guns. She and her armies have plundered planets, savaged solar systems and made Andromeda the most hated galaxy in the known universe.

"It's time," I say with a heavy sigh. "Prepare our forces to invade Earth."

Don't judge me. You don't know what happened yet. I blame Harry Handsome. It all started with him.

In case you haven't heard of him (as if!), Harry

Handsome used to be the most fancied member of top pop boy band This Way Up, whose recent split traumatised the nation. Luckily, the distraught singer was soon cheered up by his own solo success, mostly financed by my sister, Holly, who spent every waking minute listening to his soppy tunes and wallpapering her bedroom with his dopey face.

He didn't even look like he understood his own lyrics. How were we to guess he would turn out to be a secret agent in the service of the evil Emperor of Andromeda, the very Emperor who had me kidnapped as a baby so he could take over the Triangulum Galaxy—or 'home' as I had to learn to call it.

As soon as Harry Handsome announced his new tour, I knew he was up to something. Crimes against music, obviously, but also something even more sinister. His annoyingly captivating eyes were everywhere, captivating people like crazy as they gazed out of giant posters—the eyes, not the people. Whoever saw them had strange reactions, including my sister's friend who had broken her ankle falling off the pavement while staring at Harry's face gliding past her on the side of a bus. Ironically, this meant she would miss the Harry Handsome 'Follow Me' tour she and Holly had booked as she would be in hospital, collecting signatures for her massive plaster cast. Bad luck for her, but even worse for me, because Holly had decided I would take her place.

"I'm not going on my own," Holly said firmly as we got ready. "Someone needs to do the boring stuff like get drinks and queue for the toilet for me. I'm not wasting a minute that's not Harry-related."

After an initial period of extreme resistance, I had decided it would actually be a good idea to go. I wanted to see what Harry was up to. Not his new chord progressions—had he learned what one was yet?—but his progression with helping Andromeda invade Earth. Something told me he was up to his old tricks again.

"You can wear this," Holly said, shoving a t-shirt at me.

I dropped it on the floor in disgust. "Yeuch! I just touched Harry Handsome's nose!"

"You can't go to a concert without looking like a fan. It'll be weird. Everyone else will be covered in merchandise."

I picked up the t-shirt miserably. "Why does everything have to have his face all over it?"

Holly assumed a dreamy look as she surveyed herself in the mirror. She was wearing a Harry Handsome sweatshirt over a Harry Handsome t-shirt, topped with a Harry Handsome baseball cap. The look was completed by some HH socks. "Don't you think it's generous of him? 'To share the beauty of my face / And make the world a better place'?"

"No, and stop quoting his lyrics. You know what he really is. A spy for the Emperor—who, I should remind you, wants to kill us both." I flashed an angry look at his poster, and then quickly looked away as his eyes tried to draw me into their depths. Even his picture was annoying.

Holly gave me an angry glare. "He didn't mean it."

"What, didn't mean to bust the Emperor out of prison and fly off in The Big Green Spacebusting Machine? Which was *my* spaceship by the way." That was the part that really rankled. Apparently my father, the Slime King, had bought that spaceship for me for my first birthday. First it had been used to kidnap me, and then to rescue my kidnapper. It was the worst birthday present in history.

"He's misunderstood. It's all there, in his lyrics. You should listen properly some time."

"I like my food to go down and stay down, thank you very much." I pulled on the t-shirt. My own head basically now looked like a growth sticking out of the top of Harry's. How I was going to get through this concert I had no idea.

Holly looked at her watch and shivered with delight. "Oh my god. It's time."

Mary was waiting by the front door, jangling her car keys. I still called her Mary, even though she would soon be my adopted mum. She and Bill had been foster parents to us for so long, it seemed odd

to call her anything else.

"Are you sure about this, you two? Last time you saw Harry Handsome he stole a spaceship and busted the Emperor of Andromeda out of prison."

Holly looked hurt. "Mary! People make mistakes."

"Not ones like that. And I'm surprised you want to go, Jasper. You always claim to hate him."

"Jasper's seen the light," Holly said firmly.

Actually, I'd seen the darkness. In Harry's eyes. Those posters, this tour. It was all highly dodgy. But if I told all that to Mary, she wouldn't let us go.

I shrugged. "Like Holly said, people make mistakes. My mistake was that I didn't see the hidden depths in Harry's music until now."

"You always said he didn't have any depths." Mary narrowed her eyes at me. "If I had more time I'd probably try to persuade you not to go. But as usual I'm running around like a headless Venusian. Just be careful, alright?"

Phew. She had swallowed it. I was relieved. Pretending to actually like Harry for a few seconds had been almost physically painful.

"I thought Bill was taking us?" Holly asked as we got in the car.

"He was, but we've got a last-minute booking. Bill wanted to sort out the guest room. You know it's never been the same since the Featheroids of Nitscratch V were here. There are still bits of their nest stuck in the ensuite shower curtain."

Mary and Bill had had quite a bit of success renting out the spare room to various alien life forms after their old friend Flarp had left to look after Planet Gloop until I came of age. They had joined a bookings website and were regularly given five asteroid ratings, mainly due to their inexhaustible efforts to source the appropriate alien food for their guests. Mary said it wasn't that different from fostering really—messy and unpredictable.

"I forgot to tell you," Mary said over her shoulder as we left Little Blanding and took the Great Blanding Bypass to Blanderton. "I've found a venue for the adoption party. It's a lovely little hall with a nice little outdoor vegetable patch—I thought it would be perfect for your parents if they can make it, Jasper. They can chill out on a cabbage leaf if it all gets too much."

Yes, I have two sets of parents. And yes, one of those sets are slugs. It's all good though, because I'm going to have Earth parents and Triangulum parents. Or human parents and slug parents, if you want to put it another way. Mum and Dad really enjoy being slugs, which is kind of hard to understand, but after the traumatic time they had dealing with the Emperor and trying to defend Gloop I guess they've earned the right to lie around and munch on leaves all day. They are very supportive of my Earth life and promised they would try to make it for the adoption party. Maybe Flarp would bring them in her lunch box.

"That's great, Mary!" I said.

Holly had gone quiet.

"What do you think, Holly?" Mary asked. "About the venue?"

"Yeah. Fine."

"Are you still both going to help me with the catering?"

"Yes," we both groaned.

"Well thanks for the enthusiasm! This is supposed to be a big moment for us all."

"Sorry. Yes, of course I'll help," I said quickly, feeling guilty.

Holly just stared out of the window. I guessed she was too busy thinking about Harry to concentrate on anything else.

Mary pulled up on a side road near to the arena. "You'll have to walk the rest of the way. The whole place is packed with fans and I've got a new set of lodgers to prepare for. Give us a ring when it finishes. And be careful, won't you?"

"We're space adventurers now, Mary, remember?" I pointed out.

We clambered out of the car and into a stream of people. Most of them were the same age as Holly. In fact, most of them looked exactly like Holly—

dressed top to toe in Harry Handsome gear. We stepped around knock-off merchandise laid out on the pavement.

"Get me a baseball cap, would you?" I asked Holly.

Holly bought me a baseball cap for five pounds. The image of Harry was so badly printed that he almost looked ugly. Almost, but not quite.

"I knew you'd succumb," Holly said triumphantly as she handed it over. "You're a true fan now."

"It's to cover my face," I said, pulling it down low over my eyes. "I don't want anyone to recognise me."

Holly ignored me. "Ooh, look! There's the stage door—just think, Harry's behind there getting ready right now," she gushed as we approached the building.

We trooped through the bag search and into the foyer where the official merchandise was on display. Holly spent all her savings on a Harry Handsome duvet cover and pillowcase.

"Hold this," she said, shoving it at me.

"Until when?" I complained.

"Until we get home. Come on, our seats are up here."

We trudged up several flights of stairs to get to the top of the arena.

"You might have spent a bit more and got us some decent seats," I puffed as we teetered across to seats ZZ33 and ZZ34.

"He's a superstar! The concert sold out so fast, it was a miracle I got *any* tickets. These were the last seats left."

I stuffed the duvet cover and pillow case set under my seat with difficulty. "Who's the support band then?" Maybe it would be someone good who actually loved music rather than their own reflection.

Holly read aloud from her programme. "Harry's personal message to his fans says that he wouldn't dream of depriving them of himself for half the show, so there is no support band. And no backing band either. Just the pure Harry experience."

I groaned. "The pure cash experience, you mean. Harry just wants to keep all the tour money for

18

himself, to spend on his evil deeds for the Emperor."

Holly turned towards me, her eyes burning with indignation. "What if he's changed? You told Mary that people make mistakes."

"Only so she'd let us go to the concert. Harry can't change. That would involve some sort of thought process."

Holly huffed. "You wait till you hear his lyrics, then you'll understand."

"That reminds me, I didn't bring a sick bucket. Can I borrow your new pillow case? Ow!"

The lights went down before I could see if it was Holly who had kicked me, or whether I'd just banged my leg on the seat in front that was mere inches away. Never mind. If the worst came to the worst and I barfed at Harry's nauseous poetry, I had the hat.

Grimacing with pain, partly because of my leg and partly because of the ordeal to come, I made myself as comfortable as I could. There was one good thing about sitting up here. Harry would be so far away, he would be a dot. I wouldn't have to see his face at all.

A huge screen blinked into life. There was a burst of noise as five thousand people screamed and Harry Handsome's face filled half of my vision. I tried to wrench my eyes away so I could look at the tiny figure that had just walked onto the stage instead, but I couldn't. Harry's eyes seemed to bore from the giant screen right into my soul. So much for him being a dot.

The camera panned out a little as Harry picked up a guitar and climbed onto a stool in the middle of the stage. The opening chords to his latest song, 'You Will Always Love Me (And I Don't Blame You)' began, though I was surprised anyone could hear them with all the shrieking.

Even Holly was doing it. "We love you, Harry!"

"*I* love you," I said, correcting her.

She turned to me with a rapturous look. "Oh, that's so sweet. You do like him after all."

I scowled. "No, I mean—oh, forget it."

The camera was zooming in again on Harry's face, which was now in sad mode. His eyes seemed to brim with tears. It had to be make-up or something. He couldn't be that moved by his own lyrics. Maybe he had peeled some onions before coming on stage. Or, more likely, he had got someone else to peel them for him. What was worse, everyone around me was crying as well. Tears were flooding down their cheeks as they moaned out the lyrics.

I gripped the edges of my seat, feeling my nerves jangle. The next song began and suddenly everyone was smiling and clapping along as though nothing had happened. Harry seemed to be able to manipulate the crowd in any way he chose. Maybe this seemed harmless enough, but putting it together with the mesmerising effect of the posters gave it a more sinister tone.

A new song began, one I'd never heard before. The beat was strong and hypnotic. Everyone started waving one hand in the air and swaying from side to side. They looked like one entity; a field of wheat swaying in the wind. I felt an irresistible urge to join in.

"Holly!" I hissed. "Something's wrong."

"Shut up, you're ruining it," Holly hissed back. She was waving too, although I noticed she hadn't been crying like the others.

"But don't you think this is a bit weird?" I asked, as everyone stood up at the same time and raised the other hand. "It's like he's hypnotising them or something."

"This is totally normal for a concert," Holly said, as she and 4,998 other people stood on one leg.

I felt my leg twitch. It wanted to be like everyone else's legs, obeying Harry. I got up.

"I'm going to the toilet," I said, pushing past her. I had to get out of there, before I turned into one of them.

My arms were dying to wave. I sidled past the other people on the row, making them wobble on their one leg, and managed to get out onto the stairwell. The door into the auditorium shut behind me and the music softened. I sat down on the top step, feeling exhausted. The effort to resist Harry had been huge. It was like a game of Simon Says using mind control.

Mind control. Was that what Harry was up to? But why? I had to find out more. I probably had a good hour while everyone else was in there doing the hypnotic hokey cokey or whatever it was. Maybe I could get into Harry's dressing room and have a poke around?

I ran downstairs and back into the foyer. A few members of staff were milling around showing each other pictures of Harry they had taken on their phones. Remembering the stage door that Holly had spotted earlier, I slipped out of the front and around the side of the building. It was nice and cool outside. I took some big gulps of air that cleared my head of Harry's smooth, syrupy voice and pushed the stage door open. Two security guards were chatting at the end of a corridor. A big mound of presents was stacked up against the wall, which gave me an idea. I grabbed one of the larger gifts and adopted a confident walk as I approached the guards.

"Harry asked me to put this in his room," I said, deepening my voice. The present partially hid my face and I was hoping they might think I was older than I was.

"Nice try. Clear off," one of the security guards said, turning away and making sure he blocked the corridor before continuing his conversation.

Time to play the alien card.

"Okay then. How about I tell Iko Iko Iko, Son of Iko Iko, Grandson of Iko, Emperor of Andromeda Galaxy and Lots of Other Places Too that his present wasn't wanted after all?"

The guard whipped around. Both of them looked suddenly scared. The nearest one even did a little bow as he stood aside. "So sorry," he gabbled, his manner now completely different. "Please don't tell the Emperor. You won't… zap me, will you?"

I paused for dramatic effect. "We'll see."

Harry's room was just past the guards on the right. It was full of flowers, chocolates and cards. I helped myself to a few soft centres as I looked around. Trouble was, I didn't know what I was looking for. Evidence that Harry Handsome was an alien spy? I knew that already. What I needed was something that would explain his sudden interest in playing Simon Says with the contents of Blanderton Arena. I looked through the rows of cards and bunches of flowers on his dressing table. Tucked in behind a framed photo of himself I found it—a map showing the locations of every Asbi's supermarket in the country.

Doesn't sound very promising, does it? But to me it meant something crucial. The first time I went to space, it was through a self-service checkout at the Little Blanding branch of Asbi's. It was just for an alien conference mind you, but I'd still ended up coming face-to-face with the Emperor. The staff still give me funny looks whenever I go in there. Guess that's to be expected when you see someone beaming out of existence one day and buying chocolate spoons the next.

Now Harry needed to know where other branches of Asbi's were. There could only be one explanation—the Emperor was planning on using their self-service checkouts as alien portals again.

That just left the mind control stuff unexplained. There had to be a connection.

I needed to talk this over with Holly. I considered taking the map as physical evidence, but Harry would be able to get that information again quickly enough and I didn't want to give myself away by nicking anything. Hopefully he would just blame the guards for the missing chocolates. I folded the map and replaced it behind the photo of Harry. He had even signed it—to himself.

One more strawberry cream and I was out of there.

I raced back to the main entrance of the arena. I hurried across the foyer to the stairs leading to our seats—and found myself bouncing off the fluorescent-vested frontage of a member of staff.

"Ticket, please," she said, holding out her hand.

"My sister's got mine. She's inside. I just popped

out for some fresh air."

"A likely story. We've had a few like you tonight. No ticket, no entry."

"But I was in there! I can even tell you what songs he was singing."

"Name some Harry Handsome songs, can you? Like everyone else in the universe?"

"Everyone was waving their hands. He was sitting on a stool…"

"Think I was born yesterday, do you? Hop it."

"They were doing that too! Listen, something weird's going on. I think Harry's trying to hypnotise them or something. I have to stop him."

The woman rolled her eyes. "Another obsessive stalker. No wonder the lad has security wherever he goes. Now clear off."

"Fine." I walked away, then twisted back and tried to dodge past her. She was surprisingly strong.

"Sling your hook, you weirdo. Now."

Fuming, I walked off, thrashing my tail. Wait a minute—tail?

The toilets were by the door—I rushed in and examined myself with horror in the full-length mirror.

Just as I'd feared: I was changing into a giant slug.

2

TURNS OUT I'M THE
INCREDIBLE SLUG

Haven't told you that yet, have I? It's not like I'm ashamed or anything. No, being able to turn into a slug is great. I mean, it's a superpower, isn't it? I've always wanted a superpower and now I've got one. Dad (the slug one) says it's technically more of an allergy that runs in the family and has got a bit out of control, but still. I can change into something else at will. How cool is that?

Only it wasn't at will anymore. It had started to happen when I got angry. I was like the Incredible Hulk, only in slug form. The Incredible Slug. Any feeling of rage and I got the urge to wave my slug tail about, and that kicked off the transformation.

Sometimes it was just the tail. Sometimes it was more.

I checked the mirror with trepidation. Yep, looked like it was going to be the whole caboodle—antennae and all.

Being a slug had been brilliant on Planet Gloop. First, it had helped me escape from the slime mine where the treacherous Slime Minister Grek had imprisoned me so she could carry on ruling Gloop instead of Mum and Dad. That time I had been slug-sized and able to ooze through a hole in the rock. I'd even been able to transform back into a human and rescue Mum and Dad too.

Then, later on, I'd mucked up the transformation process and became giant, but it had worked out really well. I'd blasted the Emperor, his guards and Grek with super slime and bundled them into the dungeons. Grek was still in there now but I didn't feel sorry for her. My dad had made the dungeons into a chill-out zone for himself years before. Grek had a lifetime of table tennis and TV box sets to enjoy.

I'd panicked at first when I couldn't change back

into a human at will, but eventually it had happened. And anyway, the people of Gloop, who were all obsessed with slime, had loved their sluggy king. All the currency and stamps had my massive slug face on them. They had even drawn a massive outline of me on the Slime Cliffs. It looks like a crime scene after a ginormous slug has been murdered.

Being a slug wasn't glamorous at all on Earth. Mary had managed to cover for me a few times by telling the school I had a recurring disease called *Limax Maximusitis*. It had worked so far but as soon as Mrs Bodge in the office looked up the meaning of the Latin phrase she would know it meant giant slug-itis. Mary would have to do some in-depth research into rare diseases pretty soon if she was going to keep the school fooled every time I went full slug.

I heard the door to the toilets start to open behind me. I squirted out some slime to hold the incomer up a bit and oozed as quickly as I could into the nearest cubicle.

There was the sound of scrabbling feet followed by a thud, an "Ow!" and then a "Yeuch!"

I winced. Luckily I hadn't released too much slime or the person would be tangled up on the floor, just like the Emperor had been on Gloop.

Another surge of rage filled me. If it hadn't been for Harry Handsome, the Emperor would still be playing table tennis in Dad's luxury dungeons now. He'd probably be really good at it as well, what with his uncanny ability to extend his arms and deliver stinging slaps to his hapless guards.

Pop! The final piece of me turned into its slug equivalent. It was my head, which was a slightly odd sensation. I felt like I had just been pulled out of a bottle. The cubicle was pressing in around me very tightly. My eye stalks shook with frustration and I had to use all my willpower to stop my tail from banging on the floor and frightening the person in the next cubicle. Trust this to happen now, just when I was on the verge of discovering Harry's plans. I needed to be back in that auditorium to see what he was going to do next. It was so frustrating.

Slam! My tail bashed up and down in fury. Don't worry, it missed the floor. It landed in the open toilet instead, bashing a wave of toilet water into the air which rained down on my head like the worst shower ever.

"Aaargh! I hate you, Harry," I snarled.

The person in the cubicle next to me left pretty soon after that.

It seemed like I was trapped in there for hours. The only good thing was that I couldn't hear Harry's music anymore, only a dull and distant thudding and bursts of cheering. I tried to change back, I really did. I went through the seven steps, just like Dad had taught me all those months ago in the slime mine, but nothing happened.

Finally, after going through the seven steps about ten times—or was it the ten steps about seven times? I was too annoyed to think properly anymore—I heard the door burst open and the sound of someone skidding, accompanied by a loud swear word.

"Slime! Jasper, are you in here?"

Holly sounded almost relieved. You see, she does love me after all.

"Yes!" I called.

"Well come out so I can kill you."

She just has a weird way of showing it, that's all.

"I don't think I can." I unlocked the door and some of me burst out and wedged in the gap. "It's a full transformation," I explained.

"Yes, I can see that." Holly reached out to grab me, but there was nothing to get hold off. "I'll have to pull you by your eye stalks."

"No—aarrrgggggh!"

With an agonising wrench I was out. I sunk onto the floor, my eyes at the end of their antennae resting helplessly on the ceramic tiles as they tried to pop back into shape.

"It was the only way," I heard Holly say briskly. "And you deserve it. While you were in here messing around, Harry invited everyone to his after-show party. They've all gone off with him in a fleet of helicopters. Every single person apart from us."

"What!" I prised my eyeballs from the floor with a *schpluck*.

"I could have been there too—only some teeny weeny milligram of sisterly concern made me go and look for you instead."

"And they went off in helicopters?"

"Harry told everyone to go up to the roof. I heard a whirring sound."

I pulled myself upright. "Those weren't helicopters. They were spaceships! Harry's kidnapped them!"

Holly looked shocked. "Harry wouldn't do that!"

"You think? He had all of them doing the clone can-can earlier. He was hypnotising them, don't you see? And now he's got them to go with him. Listen to this. While you were busy copying him like a zombie, I was searching his dressing room."

"Oh my god! I'd die to go in his dressing room."

"I found something. A map showing the location

of all the Asbi supermarkets in the country."

"He shops at Asbi's like a normal person!" Holly marvelled. "That's so humble of him."

"Don't you remember? Asbi's is where the Emperor placed the portal. I think he's planning on doing it again. And somehow Harry's involved."

"By having a party? Which I'm not at, by the way. Don't make excuses, slime-for-brains. You've ruined my life."

"At least you've still got a life, unlike the people he's hypnotised." I tried to ooze past her. "Come on, I need to find out what's happened."

"Not like that you don't. Do you want to be put in a zoo? Here, you left your baseball cap behind." Holly plonked it on my head. My eyestalks bent out at painful angles. She looked me up and down speculatively, then sighed. "I really hate you today. But, seeing as you're going to be my brother…" She shoved the Harry bedding at me. "Put these on. They're the only thing that'll fit."

"Won't I just look like a bed?"

"It's better than looking like a slug. Now get on with it, before someone comes in."

With many unnecessary expressions of disgust, Holly helped me slide into the duvet cover. Once I was in, it was surprisingly comfy. And at least now I was on the inside of it I didn't have to look at Harry's face on the outside of it. That was for other people to suffer.

Holly took off the baseball cap and put the pillowcase over my head.

"It's almost like it was made for me," I said, moving off and bashing into the wall.

"You can have it," I heard Holly say. "I'm never using it after this."

I felt a pull and realised she was leading me out of the toilets and into the foyer. I couldn't see a thing, but I had to trust her. After all, she was my foster sister. In a few days, she would be my real, adopted sister. If I couldn't trust Holly, who could I trust?

"Ow! That felt like the wall!"

"This isn't easy, you know." Holly paused. "That's odd. I can hear the helicopters again."

I listened. There was a whirring sound and then the whole building shook slightly. Soon I could hear lots of people entering the foyer. Cautiously I stuck my eyestalk out of the bottom of the pillowcase. The Harry Handsome fans were back! I breathed a sigh of relief. They looked happy, too, chattering and laughing together. Perhaps they hadn't been hypnotised after all? The crowd began to move past us and out of the main doors.

"They look like they've had the time of their lives," Holly fumed.

"How could they? They were only gone for about fifteen minutes! Ask them what happened," I told Holly.

"Alright, but put that eyestalk back in. You look conspicuous." Holly marched off.

I slid down the wall, trying to look like a pile of crumpled bedding. I listened as people walked past me.

"That was amazing!"

38

"I never thought I'd see the inside of Harry's luxury penthouse flat!"

"He spoke to me—to *me!* It was like there wasn't anyone else in the room."

"He spoke to me as well. He's such a good listener. He told me I should get a job in Asbi's."

"Me too! It's his favourite supermarket. He said he'll come in and buy something if I'm there."

"We should go first thing tomorrow, see if there are any jobs going."

"Too right. It's what Harry would want us to do."

The voices faded out. I felt a sudden thump on me and couldn't breathe.

"It's me," Holly whispered.

"Get off! You're suffocating me!"

"It looks more realistic if I'm sitting on you. Besides, you deserve it." Holly shifted and at last I could breathe. "I just spoke to some girls. They said they'd had the time of their lives and the party had gone on for hours."

"But how could it have?"

"They also said they were all going to get jobs at Asbi's in the morning."

"That's what I heard as well."

Holly went quiet. For a moment, all we could hear were chattering voices and the words 'Harry' and 'Asbi's' coming up time and time again.

Holly sighed and started muttering to herself. "Alright. Okay. It's small scale for the Emperor, but maybe he's using it as a testing phase. First us, then the world." She took another deep breath. "I'm beginning to think you were right."

"What?"

"Don't make me say it again. It was painful enough the first time."

"Talking of pain, can you get off me now?" I grunted.

Holly got up and pulled me to my feet. Foot. I only had one now. "Let's go. I already phoned Mary. We need to tell her and Bill everything."

We made our way to the meeting place at the side street. Luckily, everyone was too full of the fake after-show party to comment on a bed walking by itself with an eye on a stalk poking out of it. Holly was just pulling out her phone to see where Mary was when there was a screech of brakes and Mary and Bill's battered old people-carrier pulled up.

Mary thrust her face out of the window. She was sweating and her hair was standing on end. "Sorry I'm late—it's chaos at home. I promised Bill I'd be five minutes at the most."

"Five minutes! But we live ten miles away," I exclaimed, pulling off my pillow case.

Mary didn't seem to notice anything different about me. "Hop in, quick."

We dived for the back seats as she revved the engine. Soon we were speeding through the streets of Blandington like a getaway car.

"Cool," I said as Mary took the corner on two wheels and careered down a narrow street.

"This is one way!" Holly yelped.

We both screamed as Mary stamped on the brakes, spun round, and accelerated off in the opposite direction.

"Where did you learn to drive like this?" I asked.

"I used to race podthrusters around Bliggleblox Centauri, back in the day."

Mary's secret past as a space adventurer was constantly surprising.

"Let's tell her about Harry when we get back," Holly said to me as our heads collided for the fourth time. "I want to get home alive."

At last, Mary screeched onto the drive. The car juddered to a halt with what sounded like a final death rasp. I flopped out onto the grass, my head spinning. It was dark now and the lights from the house lit up the lawn with a soft glow.

"I should get Flarp to modify this someday so it can cope," Mary said, giving the people-carrier an affectionate pat. It juddered again and the exhaust fell to the ground. "Make that ASAP."

I almost didn't notice the small coloured ball that came flying out of the upstairs window. It hit me on the head, and that's when I noticed it.

"Ow! What the…" It was soft and furry. I flicked it with my tail.

"Don't! Can't you see it's alive?" Holly grabbed the ball and cradled it in her arms. It squeaked and moved about. Suddenly I could make out two tiny eyes peering mischievously out of a shaggy fringe of blue fur.

"Oh asteroids! They've escaped again. Bill!" Mary yelled. She wiped a hand across her brow. "Meet the new lodger, kids."

"That's the new lodger?" I said disbelievingly as the blue ball nuzzled up to Holly.

"One of them. Here we go, look out!"

Mary was pointing up at the window. A tidal wave of fluffy balls was pouring out, aiming straight for us. I ducked. Mary started darting about, diving like a goalkeeper.

"They're all going to die!" Holly yelped, joining in.

It was an impossible job. I lay down and let them land on my big soft sluggy body. It was like being pelted with tennis balls. Painful, but not fatal.

At last it stopped. The little things were wriggling all over me.

"Look at all the different colours! They're so cute!" Holly squealed.

"Cute is one word for them. A pain in the neck is the other," Mary grumbled.

Bill emerged from the garage with a wheelbarrow. "Quick, get them in here! Before Mary sees—oh."

Mary put her hands on her hips. "I thought you said you had them under control?"

"I did! They were asleep, I swear. Don't worry, I've got this." Bill picked up one of the small round creatures and put it in the wheelbarrow. It giggled.

"And how's that going to get up the stairs? Here you are, everyone." Mary handed out some Asbi's Bags for Life. "Grab as many Fluffians as you can."

We all started loading up our bags. The Fluffians seemed to find it hilarious and rolled around the front lawn dodging through our legs. They couldn't do that to me, of course, and I got quite good at flicking them into my bag with my tail. It was a bit like golf, only with a giant slug as the bat and alien fluff monsters as the golf balls.

"I see you're a slug again, Jasper," Mary said, diving past me in pursuit of a particularly athletic specimen. "We'll have to do something about that sometime. It's probably down to all those hormones you've got rushing around and making you grumpy."

"I haven't got any hormones rushing around!" I snapped.

But Mary had descended on her Fluffian and was holding up a full bag triumphantly. "Right, back to the guest room. And this time we lock the window as well as the door. We've spent the whole evening chasing after them."

"We'll tell them about Harry's plan after this, when they can concentrate more," Holly said as we went upstairs with our bags, which seemed to be vibrating.

You're probably surprised that a giant slug can

go upstairs. Don't be. This foot is pretty good you know. It's all-terrain. The stairs are just like bumpy stones on a pavement.

Mary opened the door of the guest room and started speaking a strange language, like rustling leaves. I realised she must be wearing a GarbleGadget III, like the one I had worn at the alien conference on my first trip into space. I wondered who she was speaking to.

"I thought we'd got all the lodgers," I said to Bill as we walked into the room.

We hadn't. There was one left. It was the size of a large, soft, red beanbag. A huge, soft red bean bag. And it was snoring.

"Blimey, that's big."

"Quiet, Jasper! You'll wake it up," Mary hissed. "Lock the windows, Bill, and let's release this lot and get out before they can follow us again."

"Is that their mum?" I asked.

Mary emptied her bag. The Fluffians poured out. "I've been doing some research. Apparently they're self-cloning but technically I suppose mother is the nearest thing—oh my goodness. Stand back, everyone."

The mother, if that was the word, had opened her eyes. And her mouth. It was huge. A giant tongue emerged, long and bendy. It swept around the room and began scooping the baby Fluffians into its jaws.

"She's eating them!" Holly shrieked. "We have to do something!"

It was too late. We had all emptied our bags at the same time as Mary. Every single Fluffian had been devoured.

There was a shocked silence.

"Hang on a minute." Bill stepped bravely towards the huge fluffy creature, whose eyes were closed once again, and lifted the corner of its mouth. Some contented baby Fluffians shifted and made sighing noises as they nestled between her teeth.

We all let out a collective sigh of relief.

"It must be like a pouch," Bill said, smiling at us. "I think they'll be safe there until morning."

"You could have told us about the pouch, Mary," Holly said grouchily as we tiptoed out and Bill locked the door.

Mary looked slightly embarrassed. "I didn't get that far in my research. It was a last minute booking! We were due to have a nice old Venusian couple arriving tonight but they cancelled due to Earth allergies. I had everything set up for them, including a personalised menu which is now completely wasted. Look forward to Venusian spiceworms for the next week, everyone." She yawned. "I'm exhausted. Tell me about the concert tomorrow, kids. And Jasper, try to turn human in time for school on Monday, will you? I panicked on the phone the last time and said you had the Black Death. I think Mrs Bodge may be starting to catch on. Night all."

"We'll just have to tell them in the morning," Holly said as we trudged along the corridor to our rooms.

"But the Emperor could have his army bursting through those portals by then!" I protested.

"Look, *if* Harry is trying to get his fans to work in Asbi's—and that's a big *if*—then they need to go and get jobs there first, and that's not going to happen overnight, is it? Now shove off and wake up human. And when you do, go and put that duvet cover in the bin—or better still, an incinerator. I don't want it anywhere near me after your sluggy body has been in it."

I think she meant 'sleep well', I told myself as I oozed off to my room. Why did everyone think I could just change back to my own body at will? As if I'd stay a slug. I mean, where was the fun in that? I squirted a jet of slime and surfed along it to my room. Alright, there was a bit of fun, but nothing that made up for being a giant slug.

I curled up on the floor, my body still in the Harry Handsome duvet case. As I closed my eyes on their drooping stalks I saw Harry's face on the giant screen and his fans copying him like a zombie army. I'd stop him, even if I had to do it on my own. There was a squeak from underneath me, and I shifted. A lone blue Fluffian zoomed up and nestled under my chin, where it settled with a sigh. Okay, not quite on my own.

3

TURNS OUT VENUSIAN SPICEWORMS ARE ALIVE...

Holly and I had all day to talk to Mary and Bill, but they just weren't listening. To be fair, they were spending all their time chasing Fluffians, cooking up Fluffian recipes and chasing Fluffians again, but this was important.

"Maybe I should just talk to Flarp," I suggested.

Holly was lying on the sofa reading a magazine called 'Hunky Harry—the Inside Look'. I was lying on the floor—it was more comfortable for my sluggy body that way.

"Huh?" she said vacantly.

"You're not being hypnotised again, are you? Soon you'll be swearing nothing happened yesterday at the concert."

"What concert? Aw, look at your little slug face. I'm joking. I'm not hypnotised. But seriously—does *that* look like an evil person to you?"

She thrust the magazine at me and subjected me to a life-size close-up of Harry's face. Flawless complexion, chocolate brown eyes, swishy hair falling across his brow in just the right places…

"Yes, it does. I feel repulsed. What more evidence do you need? Don't change your mind now, Holly. You're the only other person who can stop him."

Holly sighed. "Alright then. Talk to Flarp. Ask her what we should do. Aren't you supposed to call her every day anyway?"

"Well…" Flarp had told me to call her any time to stay involved in matters on Gloop, my birth planet that she was looking after for me until I came of age and was ready to take my rightful place as king. She had even given me a special intergalactic communications device to make it all easier. I could be as involved as I wanted. The truth was, I hadn't wanted. I'd sort of enjoyed my time being king there for a few weeks, but it was a lot more enjoyable not being king. Turns out being the ruler of a planet full of slime involves a lot of ceremonial opening of the new slime mine chambers and not much else.

I squirmed off up to my room. Now where was the gizmo Flarp had given me to talk to her? I finally found it under an old sock in the corner of the room. It was a simple white cube and I hadn't a clue how to open it. After a frustrating ten minutes, I bashed it across the room with my tail. It hit the wall and a projection instantly filled the space, becoming a flickering screen. That was easy.

"Flarp?" I said cautiously.

The flickering stopped and a bleary-eyed face appeared, the skin tinged green. I recognised the slimer—short for slime miner—who had volunteered to be in charge of security when I had liberated them from being slaves of the Emperor. The job had attracted him due to the amount of down time.

"Alright there?" he said sleepily. "Oh, hello, Your Royal Greenness. I weren't nodding off, honest. Here, it's not a Code Green, is it? Only I ain't got the slime canon ready."

"No, it's not a Code Green. Is Flarp there?"

"Flarp? Nah, course not."

"What do you mean, course not?"

"Flarp ain't here. Why would she be?"

"Because she's supposed to be ruling Gloop?"

"Oh yes, that. Well, she's off visiting someone. Won't be back for ages."

I stared at the screen, fuming. Who could Flarp be visiting? She had promised to protect Gloop from the Emperor of Andromeda!

The slimer was scratching his head. "Some sort of adoption ceremony thingy."

Oh no. "She's visiting us, isn't she?"

"You? Oh yes, it were something like that. She did mention you. Only I don't know what she's going on about half the time. Alien ships this,

Andromeda that. Makes my head spin, it does."

"Great," I sighed. "Well, at least I know Gloop is in safe hands."

"Course it is, Your Royal Greenness."

"I'm being sarcastic."

"Are you? Oh dear. Well, I hope you get better soon. Goodnight—I mean, goodbye."

"Wait! When did she leave? How long would it take her to get here?"

"Back up, back up! When did she leave, you say? Well, it weren't today because I would have remembered that, so it must be tomorrow. I mean, yesterday. Or the day before. Is there a name for that?"

"I don't know. Yesteryesterday?"

"That'll do. And what was the other question?"

I spoke slowly and deliberately through gritted teeth. "How long would it take her to get here?"

"Well, that depends. If she was using the Big Green Spacebusting Machine, it would only take a few days, what with that being the fastest ship on Gloop, but of course that's not available anymore is it, as it got nicked—of course you know about that, don't you? Now if she was using the second fastest ship—not that I'm saying she was, mind you, but if she was—"

I started wrestling with the box again. In the time I had worked out how to switch him off, the slimer had given me exactly zero nuggets of useful information.

So Flarp was out of the equation too. That left just two people to stop Harry Handsome: me, and his number one fan.

Mary and Bill were so busy that they left us out a tin of Venusian spiceworms on the kitchen table for Sunday lunch, just as Mary had threatened.

"Can't we help?" I asked Mary as she tossed a tin opener at me and rushed off with a litter tray. For the Fluffians, I should add. Not us. I scooped the tin opener up with my tail from where it had fallen on the floor after bouncing off me. Mary was so busy

56

she had forgotten I didn't have hands.

"The best thing you can do is to keep yourselves occupied and let us get on with looking after the lodgers," Mary called over her shoulder as she disappeared. "Why don't you do something for the adoption party?"

Holly shoved the tin at me across the table. "Because we don't want to help with the stupid adoption party. Thanks for nothing. I'll go without."

I hoped Mary hadn't heard her.

"Before you go…" I said hopefully.

Holly glared at me as she opened the tin and poured Venusian spiceworms onto my plate. "Enjoy," she snapped, and stomped off upstairs.

Nothing got better after that. Holly went to her room and turned up Harry Handsome extra loud. I tried to enjoy my meal before squirming upstairs to sit on my bed, feeling the Venusian spiceworms wriggling through my intestines. I hadn't expected them to still be alive. Hopefully my hardy slug digestion system would cope with them. I swished my tail and the baby Fluffian bounced up and down on it and giggled delightedly.

"You should probably go back where you belong," I told it.

The Fluffian ignored me. Probably because I wasn't wearing a GarbleGadget III and it couldn't understand me. But maybe because it didn't want to go back to where it belonged, which was a giant mouth. I knew how it felt. I belonged on Gloop, really. I had been born there and kidnapped when I was a baby. Bill had rescued me and brought me to Earth. And I had decided to stay here, at least until I was older. Being adopted by Mary and Bill was making that into a firm decision. I wondered if I was worried about that, and thought about it for a bit. No, I was happy I was going to be adopted. Mary and Bill were my Earth parents and that was how I liked it. This felt like home. But then why did Holly seem so glum about it all?

I flicked the baby Fluffian into the air and oozed along the corridor to Holly's room. The poster of

Harry's face was no longer there; instead a large golden 'HH' filled the door. It was a shame; I had sort of enjoyed biffing him on the nose every time I knocked.

"Hols? It's me."

"I don't want slime in my room," Holly snarled.

"Well come out then."

The door opened. "I don't want to talk to you, or anyone."

"Then why did you open the door?"

Holly tried to close it again. I stuck my tail in the way.

"What are we going to do about *him?*" I jerked my tail at the giant poster at the end of Holly's bed, then quickly replaced my tail before she slammed the door in my face. "Hang on, doesn't that make you feel a bit weird?" I added, staring at Harry's chestnut brown eyes.

"A bit. But I can handle it."

"And how come you weren't affected at the concert, like everyone else?"

"I'm not sure. I wanted to join in, but it was easy to stop. Maybe it's because I know what he is."

"So you admit it, then. He's a secret agent for the Emperor and helping him in his plans to invade Earth. Go on, say it."

Holly looked down, a pained expression on her face.

"Oh come on! I feel like I'm the only person who believes the truth."

"What did Flarp say?"

"Nothing. She wasn't there. She's on the way to Earth for the adoption ceremony. If you don't help me, I'm going to act on my own. We have to stop him."

Holly wiped a hand across her forehead and sighed. "Alright. But I'm not going to stop listening to his music. Or looking at him. A lot." She let out a strangled cry. "It's not fair! The only thing in life that I love, and it's ruined."

"You love Mary and Bill too, don't you?"

"Yes, I suppose."

"Don't you want to be adopted? I thought you

were pleased. Is it your mum?"

Holly shook her head. "Nah." She ground a toe into the floor for a moment. "I wanted to do something. Get something. I don't know. I wanted to buy them a present, pay them back for everything they've done for us. But guess what? I saved up all my money, and then I blew the lot on Harry Handsome tickets and that stupid duvet."

"So you do love them after all! I thought you might have changed your mind." I felt a sudden weight lift off me. Not the weight of Earth being invaded by Andromeda—that was still quite heavy—but the weight of thinking Holly might not want to be my sister. I wanted to be adopted by Mary and Bill, but I wanted Holly to be as well. We were a family—it wouldn't have been the same without her.

"There's only a week to go until the party. I'll never save up enough pocket money by then."

"I've got some," I said excitedly, then stopped. "Oh no." I had spent the last few pounds on the latest Cosmic Wars battle craft. Suddenly it felt like an extravagant, selfish thing to have done. Still, it would look amazing once I had put the last layer of paint on. I just needed a bit more superglue—maybe they would have some in the centre aisle at Asbi's, they had everything there… I banged my tail on the floor excitedly. "I've got it! I know how you can earn some extra money at the last minute and stop the Earth from being invaded at the same time!" To my surprise, Holly didn't get it. "You can work at Asbi's."

"What? No way."

I took advantage of Holly's bewilderment to ooze into her room. It was a shrine to Harry Handsome but I was too wrapped up in my brilliant idea to let it bother me as much as usual. "It's perfect. You get the money *and* you get to see what's going on with Harry's Asbi plans."

"What about all those other people who'll be applying for jobs after the concert?"

"You'll get it easily, I know you will. Mrs Pardew says you're a maths genius."

"She thought she was talking about you. She still hasn't guessed I do your homework. Anyway, how do we know Asbi's even want people?"

"They always want people. They're desperate— they've even changed the employment age limit. I'll go with you if you want."

"Yeah, that's really going to help, slime-for-brains."

I thrashed my tail again. It was so frustrating being a slug.

Holly stood up. "Alright, I'll ring them. Just get your slimy bum off my carpet. But just so you know, you're not going halves with me if that's your plan."

"Halves?"

"With my present. I know what you're going to say. 'Just write my name on the label and I'll pay you back.' Well it never happens. You're going to have to think of your own present."

I grinned a sluggy grin. "I'm saving Earth, aren't I? What better present can you get?"

I oozed back to my room, feeling buoyant. I was

still a slug, but now I was a slug with a plan. That feels completely different, in case you were wondering.

Holly got an interview for Monday at four o'clock and went to Asbi's straight after school. I spent the day off 'sick' but in reality on Fluffian duty. Mary put me in charge of patrolling the back garden where I couldn't be seen. Whenever a baby Fluffian escaped, I had to take it back inside. It was fun playing with the little critters but after a while I began to feel sorry for Mary and Bill—you just couldn't get anything else done. No wonder they had retired from being foster carers. In a quiet moment, I escaped to the kitchen.

"At least they're only here until Wednesday, that's what I keep telling myself," Mary sighed as she made up some Fluffian infant nutrition milk from a powder. At least, that's what she said she was doing. It looked like frothy bubble mixture to me.

"And then will you be free?" I asked.

My favourite baby Fluffian was sitting on my head. It still hadn't gone back to its mum. Mary hadn't noticed.

"Well, unfortunately our next booking has also been changed. Instead of the Elderhead of Tuop—who we actually know and who's a lovely old head in a jar that causes no trouble at all—we've got the Greater Multessimal family of Sproing, who sound very hard work indeed. I'm beginning to think joining the SpaceBnB website was a bad idea after all. Still, at least we'll have some extra money for the adoption party and that's what's important."

"Talking about important," I began, sensing a way in. Perhaps Mary would listen to me this time. I had to tell her about Harry's plans.

Mary finished stirring and gave the mixture a taste. "Yeuch. Yes, it's perfect. Take that up to the guest room would you? Mother Fluffian should be asleep. Just pop it on the floor and back out soundlessly."

"I'm not soundless. I squelch."

"Well squelch quietly then. I need to research Sproing. Apparently the Greater Multessimal family will be travelling to us from the seventh dimension, which could be challenging. Bill's going to put some extra landing lights on the roof just in case."

I balanced the bowl of frothy stuff on my tail. I was getting quite good at using it now.

"Cheer up, Jasper. You're not worried about the Emperor, are you?"

Finally Mary was on my wavelength. "Yes," I said eagerly. "In fact I think he's got a plan to invade Earth—"

"Because if you are, it's completely unnecessary. Flarp has left Gloop extremely well-guarded and will soon be here in person. Bill and I are watching every movement in and out of Earth's atmosphere. We have things in place you know nothing about. So anything you think might happen can't."

"Even through the self-service checkouts at Asbi's?"

Mary laughed. She actually laughed. "Asbi's has

stopped using self-service checkouts—didn't you hear? They said they kept malfunctioning. Of course, we know different." She patted one of my eyestalks fondly. "Maybe if you stop worrying about things you'll be able to change back. We just want you to enjoy living a normal life as a normal boy, okay?"

"Okay," I said reluctantly, oozing out of the kitchen with the bowl of Fluffian infant nutrition milk still on my tail. Just an average day in my oh-so-normal life.

I heard a giggle and some glugging noises behind me. Fluffian junior was having a good old swim about and a feed in the food. At least someone was happy.

I reached the guest room, knocked, and pushed the door open cautiously. As I placed the bowl down, baby Fluffians streamed towards it and threw themselves in, just like me when I arrive at Blandington Aqua Adventure Park. Mother Fluffian had her back to me. She was sitting in front of a large screen and I could hear an alien voice squeaking away like a rusty hinge.

I ducked back behind the door in case whoever was on the screen could see me and peered carefully round. Having eyes on stalks is actually really useful. I could see the head of a thin worm-like creature with thick glasses peering out of the screen, which was positioned too high and mostly showed a portrait of an enormous black skyscraper that pierced the clouds and reached up into the star-speckled blackness of space. The worm's mouth was opening and closing but I couldn't understand a thing.

Luckily, Mary and Bill always kept a few GarbleGadget IIIs hung in a bag on the door ready for when they had to communicate with their guests. By flicking the bag with my tail I managed to knock one out and shove it into my mouth. For a moment, I felt a tinge of discomfort as something lodged itself into my throat and something else lodged itself into my ear; then I couldn't feel a thing. For the next week, until the device dissolved naturally into my bloodstream, I would be fluent in all forms of alien language, even Parpoid. At least, that's what the packaging claimed. I stuck an eyestalk back round the door.

"The Emperor will send a shuttle to pick you up at twenty-one hundred hours Earth time," a squeaky voice was saying. "The Emperor hopes you have been able to successfully carry out your mission. You have one more day. Do not let him down."

I looked at the Mother Fluffian, who still had her back to me. There was no response.

"Prepare to be debriefed by the Emperor personally on your return. Goodbye."

The screen began to flicker, and faded back into an innocuous piece of peeling wallpaper. So what did this all mean? Had the Emperor sent the Fluffians in order to cause trouble? But why? It hit me with the force of a baby Fluffian leaping out of a window. To keep Mary and Bill distracted, of course.

Talking of being distracted, I had taken my eye off the Mother Fluffian. It turned around and froze as it caught sight of me. Its beady little eyes brightened up and two thick furry eyebrows lowered in fury. I started backing away soundlessly.

Squelch!

Mother Fluffian charged towards me, knocking several babies out of the way. So this was how it was all going to end—scoffed by a giant ball of fluff. I closed my eyes and prepared for my doom. I heard munching noises. It had started already and I wasn't feeling a thing. Maybe being eaten alive wasn't as unpleasant as it was made out to be?

I risked opening one eye. The Mother Fluffian was devouring the food in greedy gulps. And it was Fluffian food, not me. I whizzed out of the door and closed it quietly behind me, panting with relief.

Those Fluffians were a nightmare—a deliberate one. The evidence was mounting up. The Emperor and Harry were planning something, and it was going to happen very soon.

4

TURNS OUT I'VE HAD
MOON STROKE

"Jasper!"

As I leant on the locked door, relieved to have escaped the jaws of Mother Fluffian, Holly thundered up the stairs.

Actually, she'll kill me for saying that. Let's try again.

Holly danced lightly up the stairs.

"I've got something to tell you!" I cried, oozing towards her.

"Shut up. I've got something to tell you that's better. I got the job, and guess who else was there too? Everyone from the concert."

"Everyone?"

"Well, three of them. The new manager gave us all jobs. Said the previous staff had all left with PTSD."

"Who's he?"

"Post-Traumatic Stress Disorder. They reckoned they'd seen two people disappear into the self-service checkouts. Which have now been banned for causing 'hallucinations'."

That was us, of course. "This is great. So when do you start?"

"Tomorrow. I'm doing four till seven every day. By the end of the week I'll have enough money to buy Mary and Bill something. Not a lot as the pay is terrible, but something."

"Did you talk to the others?"

"Yes, unfortunately." Holly rolled her eyes. "All they could do was drone on about Harry Handsome. Imagine having to put up with one of them all day."

"Yeah, imagine. That's brilliant, Hols. We'll soon find out what's going on."

"I will, you mean. It's alright for you. All you do

is sit around being a slug."

"It's not my fault. It's my hormones!" I protested.

"I've tried that one with Mary a million times. It doesn't work."

I quickly told her about what I had overheard. To my surprise, Holly didn't seem as amazed as I was.

"That would make sense," she mused.

"Do you think that website Mary and Bill use has anything to do with it? SpaceBnB?"

"Who knows? When did you say the Fluffians were leaving?"

"Wednesday. But another lot are arriving instead. The Family of Something. Mary's not looking forward to it. The Emperor is distracting them from something and it's working. It's going to happen any moment, I know it is."

We looked at each other apprehensively. It was us versus the alien invaders. We would just have to pull together and work as a closely-knit team. We were the only people who could stop Harry. Talking of which…

"Why are you still wearing your Harry Handsome t-shirt?" I demanded.

Holly pulled her jacket collar together defensively. "I'm not."

"I can see his hair. It's got so much gel on it, I'm surprised it's not served up with ice cream."

"You can talk, slime central."

Yep, we were one single-minded alien-fighting unit.

★★★

It was hard, but all I could do was wait for Holly to complete her first shift at Asbi's and report back. Tuesday really dragged. I was still off 'sick' but Mary had decided I shouldn't spend so much time in the garden as the neighbours had panicked after a fleeting glimpse of me through their upstairs window and started throwing slug bait over the fence. To make the time pass, I decided to try everything I could to turn back into a human but there was absolutely no change. Maybe it was because I didn't have access to slime? In desperation, I locked myself in the bathroom and filled the bath up with all the gunky goo I could find in there: shower gel, hair gel, moisturiser, conditioner, zit cream—you name it, I squirted it. Bracing myself, I slid in. It was freezing and I let out a strangulated cry for help which Mary and Bill were thankfully too busy to hear. Getting the stuff off afterwards was a nightmare too. I ended up so slippery that I was stuck in the bath; every time I tried to get over the side, I flopped back in.

"I hate you, Harry," I muttered to the bathroom ceiling.

It wasn't Harry's fault I was a slug. I just hated him.

Still, now I had bathed in my DIY slime, maybe the slug transformation would work. I finally managed to flop out of the bath and went through the steps just as Dad had taught me. Well, not just as he had taught me as that was quite a few weeks ago and I didn't have a photographic memory. In fact, come to think about it that was probably why it wasn't working in the first place. It wasn't the stupid hormones at all. Mary was completely wrong about that.

Nothing. "Aaargh!" I cried, rolling my eyes in their eyestalks.

I heard a giggle from the corner of the room. It was that baby Fluffian again. It didn't seem to want to leave me alone.

"I thought you'd gone back to Mumzilla," I told it.

It zoomed towards me and started bouncing up and down on my tail.

"Go on, then," I sighed. At least someone was having a good time.

There was a bang on the door.

"Jasper! We're one Fluffian short! Have you seen it?" Mary sounded panicked.

"It's fine, I've got it here." I unlocked the door.

Mary was panting. Her hair was sticking up. "Thank goodness. Apparently they can attack completely randomly."

"Attack?" I laughed derisively. "I don't think that's going to happen. We're best buddies now—

look!" I tossed the little creature up into the air with my tail. It let out a shriek of delight.

Mary groaned with despair. "That's not it! The mother's the one we're looking for!"

"What?" I sent the baby Fluffian flying.

"Someone didn't lock the guest room door properly. The adults rarely move unless they feel some powerful emotion. Love, for example. Or anger. Looks like our Mother Fluffian is on the move."

Whoops. I dived for Mother Fluffian's long lost offspring. "Could she be looking for this?" I gulped, holding it up with my tail.

"Oh, Jasper. They're not toys, you know."

"I know that! It's Fluffy who thinks *I'm* the toy."

"You've even named it."

"Only for convenience. I obviously haven't spent any time on it. I'll help you look for the mum." Actually, I had spent time thinking of a name—most of the day, in fact—but when something's that fluffy it's hard to call it anything else.

"Don't approach it," Mary warned as I squirmed

past her.

"Then how can I help you catch it?"

"You don't. You tell me or Bill and we come after it with a net."

"A special net? You're well prepared."

"A net curtain," Mary admitted. "I only hope it does the trick."

Slowly and quietly, I began to ooze my way round the house, pausing at every corner and peeking round with an eyestalk. I imagined I was James Bond, secret agent. I was Secret Slug. "I like my slime shaken, not stirred," I drawled to myself, straightening an imaginary bow tie.

"What was that, Jasper? Have you found her?" Bill yelled up the stairs.

"Er, no. Nothing yet!" I called back. Fluffy was stuck to my tail. "Come on, Fluffy. You should be able to find your mum. In fact, maybe it's better that you do. Alone." I detached the little creature by flicking it onto the floor. It looked up at me enthusiastically. I gave it a nudge. "No more play.

Go on. Find Mum. Please?" If the Mother Fluffian was enraged by the loss of her child, she would be even more enraged at the person (or slug) who had that child. It wouldn't be me. I tried to roll Fluffy along the floor like a mini bowling ball, but it just circled back and rolled up onto my tail again.

"Fine. Get me killed. You won't have your favourite toy to play with then, will you?"

"Don't worry, Bill's found it," Mary called, running up the stairs.

She beckoned me over to the landing window. Down below in the back garden, Bill was running round in circles while the Mother Fluffian hurtled after him, its mouth wide open.

"It's twice the size!" I gasped.

"Yes, they expand when they're angry."

"And it's roaring."

"Make that very angry."

I looked at Mary. "Aren't you going to help him?"

Mary smiled grimly. "Bill left that door unlocked. I'll just let him have a few more laps."

I didn't like to correct her. Mary was one tough ex-space adventurer. "I think we should get the net. Put Bill out of his misery."

Eventually Mary agreed. Turns out she had the net with her all the time. We dropped it out of the window and it landed neatly over the Mother Fluffian. Bill pulled the ends together, rendering her immobile. This seemed to calm her down and, by the time we got down into the garden, she was half the size and passive again.

Bill wasn't. "I thought I was going to die!" he managed between gulps of air.

Mary patted him reassuringly. "Fluffians don't kill unless they can see no alternative."

"She couldn't see anything through that fur! I tell you, I was a goner." Bill took Mary's hands in his and gazed into her eyes. "You saved my life, Mary. How many times is it now?"

"Five. But who's counting?"

"Ahem," I coughed. "It took two of us to throw that net down. And Mary wasn't in any hurry."

They ignored me.

"As if I would do anything else," Mary crooned. Phew. She did love him really.

We all pushed Mother Fluffian back up the stairs. It was a good job I was there or they would have struggled. Not that they admitted that. In their minds, I was still a skinny, short-for-his-age eleven year old boy. With the Black Death. Which reminded me.

"What did you tell Mrs Bodge was wrong with me this time?" I asked Mary.

Mary clapped a hand over her mouth. Mother Fluffian slipped back a step and we all nearly tumbled over. "I forgot to phone the school today! And it's gone four!"

Everyone jumped as the doorbell rang.

"This is good timing," Bill said, heaving on the net.

"I can do it by myself," I insisted. "I'm a giant slug."

"I'm not leaving you in charge of this beast," Mary argued. "Someone could die!"

The doorbell rang again. Then the letter box

opened and a voice called through, "Mr and Mrs Clarkson? It's Miss Pardew here from the school. I'm just calling round to see if Jasper is alright?"

Everyone looked at me, even Mother Fluffian through her netted bonds.

"Get out of sight!" Mary hissed.

"I will! Just let me take her up. I can do it!" I insisted.

The doorbell rang again.

"Alright, just be careful," Mary said, looking extremely reluctant.

It would be so much easier without them. "What are you going to say to her?" I asked.

Mary shrugged. "Who knows?"

I didn't envy her. I left them to it.

Once I had Mother Fluffian upstairs, I could simply roll her to the guest room. The trick was keeping the net on. I pushed her inside the room and, while the babies streamed towards her, considered my options for escape. Should I pull the net off, as though revealing the results of a magic trick, and risk being the object of her revenge? Or should I just retreat while I was still capable and let her untangle herself?

I was saved from making a hasty decision by the appearance on the wall of the flickering screen I had seen last time. I threw myself down on the floor behind Mother Fluffian, hoping I was out of sight, and felt Fluffy climb onto my head as I held my breath and listened.

"Calling codename Chaos, calling codename Chaos, do you read me?" said the voice from the screen.

I was glad the GarbleGadget hadn't worn off—I could understand every word.

The Fluffian gave a shake and threw off its netting as the little worm appeared on the screen, her glasses teetering on the edge of her—well, she didn't have a nose, so no wonder they were teetering.

"Ah, there you are," she squeaked. "I trust you achieved your aim of maiming one or both of your hosts? Good. The pickup arrangements are unaltered. Be on the roof of the building at twenty-one hundred hours Earth time. You will be taken straight to the Emperor for debriefing. I hope he is pleased with you, for your sake."

I realised this would be a good moment to retreat before Mumzilla spotted I was there. I began to slide backwards. Fluffy was still on my head. It was time for my little parasite to go home. "Get off, can't you?" I hissed, trying to dislodge it with a subtle shake.

"Our plans are proceeding well," the worm was continuing. "The portals have been put in place and will be opened by the Emperor himself at the same time all over the country. If this test phase succeeds, then…" There was a pause as though the worm was listening. "A reward? I'm afraid that will be up to the Emperor. No, you cannot have your own county on Earth. Duchess of Cornwall? Certainly not! Goodbye!"

"Get off!" I muttered to Fluffy. It seemed to be stuck to me like glue. I wondered if maybe I hadn't washed all the goo off from earlier and it was literally stuck. I batted it with my tail and it finally let go. I squirmed back through the door, closed it quietly and locked it, breathing a sigh of relief. The Mother Fluffian was safely back in her room, trying to become Duchess of Cornwall. And so was Fluffy. Safely back in the room, I mean, not trying to become Duchess of Cornwall. And I had learned more about the Emperor's intentions at the same time.

The portals were all going to be opened at once. Was he going to send through his armies? It was a terrifying thought. But how could we stop him? He was on Andromeda, and Holly and I were here. If only I had the Big Green Spacebusting Machine! But even if I had, I couldn't drive a spacecraft anyway. I was just kidding myself.

Who else had a spaceship? Flarp! And she was on her way here! And she was the Slayer of the Multi-Headed Muck Monster of Murg and all-round space hero. If only I knew when the portals were going to be opened. And when Flarp would get here.

By the time she arrived, it could be too late.

I oozed over to the top of the stairs. I could hear low voices in the living room. I flowed halfway down and stiffened as I heard my name.

"… a very vivid imagination," Mrs Pardew was saying. "At one point, he pretended he was an alien. I believe he even dyed his hair green!"

She was so close to the truth.

"Have you considered, Mr and Mrs Clarkson, that he might be trying to avoid lessons with these rather unconvincing illnesses? Is there anything going on at home I should know about?"

There was a long pause as Mary and Bill rummaged around in their brains for possible answers.

"The truth is…" Mary began.

"Yes?"

"The truth is that, well…"

"Go on."

It was so tempting at that moment to burst in and shout out, "I'm a slug!" possibly accompanied by a song and dance routine, but I couldn't have done that to Mary and Bill. I waited to see what ailment Mary could invent next instead.

"Yes, Mrs Clarkson?"

"The truth is that he's been having some hormonal problems..."

I couldn't take it anymore. I grabbed the Harry Handsome duvet cover and pillowcase that were waiting for incineration, shoved myself into them and glided into the living room—with a subtle eyestalk poking out where Mrs Pardew couldn't see.

"Jasper!" Mary gasped.

Mrs Pardew dropped her biscuit into her tea with a soggy *splok*. "Is that him in there?"

"Hello Mrs Pardew. I've got mumps. That's why I'm not in school."

"Mumps?"

"Yes. Extra large mumps. I've swelled up so much the only things that'll fit me are a duvet and pillowcase. So you see, I can't leave the house."

"Your foster parents just said you had moon

stroke," Mrs Pardew said.

"Bill said it," Mary pointed out. "Not me."

Bill looked uncomfortable. "It's like sun stroke, only from the moon."

"Oh yes, I've got that, obviously," I agreed, making it sound like the most normal thing in the world. "I've had moon stroke for *ages*. No, I thought you meant what *new* thing had I got. Yeah, the moon stroke is really bad too. It really makes my…" I looked to Bill for guidance. He made little walking motions with his fingers. "It makes my fingers hurt. So I can't hold a pen." Bill was shaking his head. "No? Oh, legs! It makes my legs hurt. I can't walk. That's why I look like I'm sliding. Oops." I collapsed dramatically on the carpet. "I thought I was getting better there for a moment, but I'm not. Extra large mumps crossed with moon stroke is really, really bad."

Mrs Pardew was looking at me in confusion. "I've never heard of moon stroke."

"No, you wouldn't have. It's rare. Ridiculously

rare," Mary said, stressing the 'ridiculous' and giving Bill a furious glare. I thought she was being a bit unfair what with claiming I had the plague the other week.

"But mumps is serious." Mrs Pardew stood up. "I'd better leave. Don't want to pick up germs and infect the rest of the school."

As Mrs Pardew stepped over me, looking slightly horrified, I congratulated myself on having thought up a perfectly legitimate illness. I even smiled at Mary, but she didn't look quite as happy as I'd expected.

Mrs Pardew made it to the door and paused. "Of course, I've never heard of anyone having mumps twice. He had it a couple of years ago as well, didn't he?"

"Yes," Mary said through gritted teeth. "He did." Whoops.

As soon as seven o'clock came, I lay in wait for Holly to come back from Asbi's. The evening's tin of Venusian spiceworms and a tin opener were ready on the table. Bill was up on the roof installing new landing lights while Mary was in the office researching Sproing. I had two bowls ready and was just wondering whether I could get into the tin just with brute force when Holly arrived with a fully loaded Asbi's for Life bag.

"Earth food!" I yelled as she unpacked a tin of beans.

Holly looked serious. "It's worse than we thought, Jasper."

"You mean, they're not Timz?" Timz Beanz were my favourite and nothing else tasted the same.

"I mean, the worst is happening. But let's eat our meal first. It could be the last one we ever enjoy."

That sounded worrying, and sort of distracted me from the fact that the beans were Asbi's own brand, or 'Jimz' as they called themselves. Another distraction was that Holly made everyone beans on toast, even Bill and Mary, and took theirs over to them. Holly never made dinner. I felt slightly jealous of Bill who would be eating beans on toast on the roof, which sounded very exciting.

I pushed a pile of beans into my mouth with my tail. Holly winced. "I hate you eating as a slug."

"Sorry," I mumbled, my mouth stuffed with beans.

"Anyway. Listen to this. All the checkouts at Asbi's are new, delivered last week. No one was expecting them. So chances are they've been tampered with."

"By Emperor Jellybutt."

"You said it. We were all trained on them today. No self-service this time, fully operated. Asbi's are making a big thing of it, by the way. 'Staffed by humans' is their new motto."

"Sounds better than 'staffed by Harry's hypnotised zombies' I suppose. These Jimz taste like cardboard—I wonder how they managed to extract the flavour?"

"Just get on with it. It's disgusting watching your sluggy tail get covered in beans. Anyway, the other three all went along with the training, but as soon as we were left on our own at the tills, they did something to them."

"What?"

"Don't you want that toast cut up?"

"Nah, I prefer it all in one. Go on."

"Well, I couldn't quite see what they were doing. But now there's a little door round the side, where we sit. You can't see it from the outside, but something—or someone—could get in. Or out." Holly let out a strangled yell of frustration. "Aargh! If only we knew!"

"Can't you just ask them?"

"It's impossible. They just block you with tales of Harry and how great the party was. The non-existent party. They're so convincing, they're making me jealous. Harry must have implanted all those memories into their minds. There's no way they all had an hour's private conversation with Harry and a swim in his pool before being the first to hear his new song."

I told her what I had found out about the Emperor

controlling the portals.

"When's Flarp coming?" she asked, expertly slicing her bread and picking up a forkful of beans on toast with a fluid dexterity I could only dream of.

"Who knows? Maybe I should try Gloop again and see if they've heard any more from her."

"We have to contact her. We've done our bit now—we know the plans. Flarp can organise someone to get to the Emperor somehow and stop him activating the portals."

I didn't say anything.

"Jasper? Come on. There's nothing more we can do. We have to let Flarp take it from here."

"I was thinking we could go with her."

"To Andromeda? You're kidding, right? We need to tell her before she gets to Earth. Every second counts. She won't have time to come and pick up a useless giant slug."

I could see Holly's point. But I didn't want to. "We could help. We were great last time. We captured the Emperor all by ourselves."

Holly put down her fork. "You were great, Jasper. And yes, we did it. But that doesn't mean it should always be us."

"I've got a superpower. I was a super slug. I still am! What better time to confront the Emperor, and this time make sure he stays in captivity for good?"

"Jasper, I understand. The Emperor kidnapped you when you were a baby. He took you away from your family. No wonder you're angry with him. But Flarp has a spaceship, weapons, contacts—she doesn't need us. And she'll be faster without us. Go and see if you can contact her. I'll do the washing up. What's that blue thing on you?"

"Fluffy, how did you get there?"

"Put that back as well. Cheer up, Jasper. We're saving the Earth here. It's just not as dramatic as last time, that's all."

Holly was right. What was I thinking? We were still doing our bit. It was time to call in the big guns, or Flarp as we called her. I oozed up to my room, Fluffy clinging to me like Velcro, and found the white cube. Lethargically, I threw it against the wall. The same slimer appeared looking as bleary-faced as last time.

"Yep? Oh, it's you again. I'm rubbing me eyes so I can keep an eye on the kingdom better, not because I've just woken up. Alright, Your Royal Greenness?"

"I've been better. Any word from Flarp?"

"Ain't she with you yet, then? Hang on, I'll have a look at me records. Oh yes, she did leave a message, so it happens. Looks like a distress call. Oops. Probably should have got back to her about that."

"What? When did she leave a distress call?"

"Not sure on that one. I don't tend to write down dates. Saves time."

"But what about saving lives?"

"What lives?"

"Flarp?" I suggested, flicking my tail impatiently.

"Oh yes. I nearly forgot about the distress call again! That wouldn't do at all, would it?" The slimer chuckled, amused by his own incompetence. "We'd better send out some help."

"Can you give her a message?"

"Nah, can't do that Your Royal Greenness."

"It's urgent!"

"Nah, I physically can't. Communications are down, you see. Distress call, then nothing. She's off grid."

"So how are you going to rescue her?"

"Don't know, but I suppose it's worth a try, isn't it?"

I shook my head in despair. No wonder the Emperor and Grek had been able to take over Gloop so easily. Without Flarp there, how long would they last?

I ended the call with an extra hard throw at the wall. Now there was even more to worry about. Earth *and* Gloop. Not to mention Flarp herself. She might look like my old partially deflated space hopper, but she was my parents' best friend. I felt a surge of anger, like a bolt of lightning charging me up. My tail thrashed angrily. It was time to act. No more dithering. And there was only one way left.

"It's nearly time for you to go home," I told Fluffy. "And I'm coming with you."

5

TURNS OUT WE SHOULD HAVE WORN SUITS

"You're what?" Holly shrieked, forgetting she had banned me from her room.

"I'm stowing away with the Fluffians. They have a debriefing with the Emperor. Once I'm there, I'll find the mechanism to open the portals and I'll destroy it. Or destroy him. Whichever I can get to first."

"That's not a plan. It's a very vague idea that won't work because you're a giant slug."

"Come with me then."

"Last time I came with you into space I had to pretend to be your servant. Correction—there was no pretending involved. I *was* your servant. Then I was Grek's servant. It wasn't exactly fun."

"You enjoyed poisoning Grek. You told me."

"Only because she was so vile. Anyway she was only briefly unconscious, worse luck. No, this is too dangerous, Jasper. We have to tell Mary and Bill."

"But this is my adoption present to them! Life itself!"

"Yes, and they're more likely to live until the adoption if we tell them." Holly sighed and shook her head. "We *have* to tell them. Even if it means shouting it in their faces." She marched out and I followed reluctantly. "Mary! Bill!"

The attic stairs were pulled down. Holly climbed up them and I flowed up after her. A step ladder was in the middle of the room and the hatch above hung open. I caught a glimpse of strange colours and bright lights. Holly climbed up to the top of the step ladder and stuck her head out.

"Stay right where you are, Holly! Don't move!" Mary's panicked voice screeched.

"What is it?" I called, squishing up onto the step ladder and forcing my head out of the hole next to Holly.

"Jasper! Whatever you do, don't move an inch!"

We were in a sort of dome made up of a network of lights. Mary's voice was coming from a huge red and green head that seemed to be floating over us. It was like looking at something designed for 3D glasses without wearing the glasses. I felt sick.

"I'm in the seventh dimension," Mary explained. I say 'explained' but it didn't actually explain anything.

Then a warped face came floating towards her, its voice distorted and weird.

I'm in the eighth. But I'm hoping I can go back down a haddock very soon.

It wasn't so much a voice as a feeling inside my mind.

"Bill? Is that you?" I asked.

Manta ray, Bill seemed to say, nodding.

"The eighth dimension doesn't translate very well," Mary added.

"What's going on?" Holly demanded.

"We've set up this dimension gate in order to ease the transition from the seventh dimension to the third, for the visiting Sproings," Mary explained. "Only it's not as easy as it says in the instructions. If either of you make a sudden gesture, the whole web will be broken and I could be trapped in the seventh dimension forever."

"What about Bill?" I asked.

"Bill could be trapped in the eighth." Mary lowered her voice. "Between you and me, I think he already is. This is really serious, you two. Whatever you need us for, can it wait?"

Holly paused. I nudged her and the step ladder wobbled.

"Don't make any sudden movements, Jasper!" Mary squealed.

"Sorry. Yes, it can wait. Can't it, Holly?"

"Yes, alright," Holly said reluctantly.

"We need to ask you to do something," Mary said, becoming smaller and then larger again. It was making my eyes go funny. "Can you round up the Fluffians and take them to the collection area over there?" She nodded her head towards a large painted square on the roof. "The mother should be fine now she's calm. Just don't make her angry."

"Most kids just have to clean their rooms at weekends," Holly complained.

"Yes, or empty the dishwasher," I agreed, swishing my tail.

"Don't!" Mary yelled.

"Sorry. We'll get the Fluffians. Good luck with the dimension stuff."

Fish, Bill seemed to say.

We returned to the landing.

"Do you think we'll ever see Bill again?" Holly asked.

"I like him as he is," I said, making some slime to skid along to the guest room. "Did you see all the colours in his eyebrows? Eighth Dimension Bill is cool."

"Wait there," Holly said. I stood outside the Fluffians' door while she nipped to her bedroom. When she came back she had her Harry Handsome jacket on.

"So. Looks like we're really going to do this," she said.

"You mean you're coming with me?" I was so pleased I almost hugged Holly, which would of course have been a huge mistake. "Want to take anything?" I asked instead.

Holly shook her head. "Saving Earth is more important than possessions."

"You've already packed, haven't you?"

Holly hoisted a small backpack onto her shoulder. "Never go into space without a toothbrush and spare underwear. What about you?"

"Oh, I'll just turn mine inside out. Here, you'd better wear one of these."

I unboxed a GarbleGadget III and passed it to her. While she popped it in, I unlocked the Fluffians' door. Mother Fluffian was awake and seemed unsurprised to see us; she opened her huge mouth and the babies flowed in obediently.

"Time to go home," I said, nodding and smiling reassuringly. "Go on, now's your chance," I urged

Fluffy, but the little creature had disappeared.

"It's probably already in the mother's mouth," Holly said. "Everything else is. I'm sure there were more pot plants in here last week. Come on, I think it will follow us."

The Mother Fluffian certainly seemed far more biddable now. Maybe it was relieved to be going home. It can't have been much of a fun trip, just being a receptacle for a mouthful of troublemakers, even if they were its own children. When we got to the attic, it even let me pick it up with my tail and pass it to Holly to push up the step ladder.

I squirmed up as well and we guided the Fluffians to the pickup spot, as directed by Mary and Bill.

Speaking of which…

"Mary! Bill!" Holly called. "Are you okay?"

The network of lights that had made up the dome was now floating in a flat grid suspended a metre or so above the roof. There was no sign of any faces, warped or otherwise. It was like our soon-to-be-parents had been stowed away in a reverse version of a piece of flat-packed furniture.

"Oh no. They're trapped in another dimension! Mary! Bill!" I yelled at the grid. "Come back!"

Holly took my arm. "There's nothing we can do. Maybe they're safer there, for now. If the Emperor's going to invade Earth, where would you rather be? Or, more likely, they've packed up for the night and are sitting in front of the TV watching *Cash Bargains Under the Hammer* with a cup of tea."

"I'll check," I began.

Holly's grip tightened. "No time! Look!"

In the now dark sky, a small dot was swiftly enlarging into a ring of lights. We hid behind the chimney as a small round spaceship touched down just in front of the Fluffian. A circular hole opened in the side and a ramp popped out.

Mother Fluffian, with her mouthful of babies, rolled up the ramp and disappeared.

"What's the plan—shall we just follow?" I whispered.

Holly pointed at the ship. "There's another door lower down. See? Must be for luggage or something. Once the main hatch has closed, we'll make a run for it."

"Did you see how quickly that thing arrived? It'll be off in seconds. We'll never make it."

"Slime!"

"I feel exactly the same."

"No, I'm not swearing. I mean, make a slime trail. We can skid along it. It'll speed us up—it's the only way."

It was a pretty good idea—not that I told Holly that. I squirted us a path and, as the main door closed, we surfed towards the ship. Secret Slug was back in business. Holly pulled open the hatch and crawled in. It was very small. She grabbed me and pulled me through with a *pop*.

We were in a teeny tiny space with just a few provisions, packed to feed passengers on long haul space journeys. Luckily, there was a good way to make extra room for ourselves—eat the provisions.

As we took off, I began to feast my way through Space Sausages, Turbo Sweets and Nova Nuts. Despite being a slug, I hadn't developed my slug parents' taste for leaves yet, thank slime.

Holly drew her knees into her chest. Her head was touching the ceiling even though she was sitting down. It was alright for me. I could just lie there in a long line.

"Great. Trapped in a luggage compartment with Swamp Thing," she groaned.

"Galactic Gob Stopper?"

"No thank you. Anyway, they don't work."

"What do you mean?"

"You're still talking."

It was great to have some quality time with Holly. The journey soon passed—although Holly said it took ages—and we felt ourselves slow down and hover. A polite but forceful voice reverberated through the small ship.

"All hail Iko Iko Iko, Son of Iko Iko, Grandson of Iko, Emperor of Andromeda Galaxy and Lots of

Other Places Too. You are now entering Andromeda, the greatest galaxy in the Local Group. Random stop and search is in operation. Also, all returning citizens must bring a holiday souvenir for the Emperor. No fridge magnets or tea towels."

"If we're stopped, we're done for," I said gloomily.

We crossed our fingers—well, Holly did, I crossed my eyestalks—and it seemed to work because eventually we were moving again. Soon we heard announcements that we were entering AndroSphere, the capital planet, and finally AndroCity itself, where a new voice hailed us.

"Welcome to AndroCity, the commercial heart of the Andromedan Galaxy and home of Tyrant Towers, the Oppression Obelisk, the Intimidation Institute and the Association of Autocrats. Please leave your integrity in the lockers at the spaceport. Thank you for your enforced cooperation."

The spaceship came to a halt, making me drop my packet of Galactic Goo Balls all over the floor, and then we heard the mechanism for the main door and ramp working.

"Now!" Holly whispered.

We pushed open the hatch and plopped onto the ground, just in time to see Mother Fluffian zoom into a clear glass lift. In a flash, the lift shot sideways off the side of the roof and disappeared into a mass of skyscrapers.

"Flying lifts!" I exclaimed, impressed.

"Wow," Holly breathed. "Look. We're so high."

We were on the roof of what had to be a massively tall building, only there were even more massively tall buildings all around so it was hard to tell. Everywhere was glass and metal as floor upon floor of office space reached up into the sky—which impressively had three suns. As for the ground, it didn't seem to exist anymore.

Every so often a glass and metal lift came whizzing past, shooting around the corners of buildings like a slalom skier. Suddenly one attached itself to a nearby skyscraper and we saw some tiny aliens step across into the building.

"So... that seems to be how people get around here," I said, as the lift picked up some new passengers, slid down a few floors, and then suddenly took off again.

We fell silent as we both realised at the same time what we had to do next.

"Mary would call them death traps," Holly pointed out.

"Maybe, but they're not as big a death trap as Earth is right now with the Emperor aiming his... whatever he's aiming at it." Still, I didn't move.

"After you, then."

"No, after you. I insist."

Holly stood up reluctantly, then threw herself to the floor as the spaceship we had arrived in suddenly took off vertically and disappeared.

"Things move fast around here, don't they?" I commented.

"The only thing that doesn't is you." Holly got up again and brushed herself down. I noticed that she checked her Harry Handsome t-shirt for scuff marks. "Don't make me pull your eyestalks again."

We walked to the edge of the roof where the lift had collected the Fluffians. I wished we had gone with them. Surely they wouldn't have betrayed us to the Emperor? Or would they? I remembered how much Mother Fluffian wanted to be Duchess of Cornwall.

"Maybe there's a call button or something," I suggested, looking around. "Oh look, there's a lovely round green cushion for me to sit on."

"Look out!" Holly screeched.

This time we both threw ourselves backwards as a lift shot out from behind a building and slammed itself down in front of us.

"That *was* the button," Holly hissed, grimacing in pain.

I wasn't grimacing in pain. I had a nice flat sluggy bottom to fall onto. "Good job I found it then, wasn't it?" I said happily. Well, almost happily. I still had to ride in the thing.

"Let's get it over with," Holly said, guiding me in with her foot. Kicking me, if you want to know the truth.

Inside it was like a normal lift but with glass windows, a glass ceiling and a glass floor. So basically not like a normal lift at all. Imagine levitating.

"Just press the button. Tyrant Towers. Quick," I urged Holly. "I feel like my insides are going to fall out, and you don't want to see a slug's insides, believe you me."

I had never said 'believe you me' before, but Bill said it sometimes and it made me feel better.

Holly pressed the button with her annoyingly useful human fingers. Instantly the lift swooped away with us in it and I was pressed up against the glass with my sluggy flesh squished into a corner of the lift.

"I've gone geometric!" I mumbled. "My face is square!"

"Mmmhhhhmmm!" Holly replied.

"What?"

"I said, get your giant sluggy foot out of my face!"

"Oh, sorry."

After freeing Holly, I decided to let the lift tip me back into the corner as it meant I was stable and could actually look out rather than spending my time bouncing off the walls. It also kept my face from looking down—thank slime—as my eyestalks were squished as well. Instead I stared at the skyscrapers, admiring the crystal-clear glass and the occasional glimpse of Andromedans sitting at desks in front of computers, or around long tables in meeting rooms, each one of them slaving away to help the Emperor increase his vast territories. There was obviously a lot of admin involved at this level of evil.

Suddenly we dived around a corner and I saw an enormous skyscraper, so tall I couldn't see the top. It was matt black, with panels where the windows were, and thick girders criss-crossed its length like an exoskeleton.

"I wonder if that's..." began Holly, as our lift

shot towards it.

CLANG! We attached to one of the girders and began moving upwards.

"...Tyrant Towers," Holly finished.

We were still moving. Up and up we climbed, until all we could see were clouds around us and the side of the building.

"It makes sense what we're doing, doesn't it?" I said eventually. The clouds were clearing and now it seemed to be getting dark. "I mean, why wait all our lives for the Emperor to come and find us? We might as well go and find him instead. Right?"

"Might as well," Holly said casually. "Is it night-time, by the way?"

I stared out of the window. "I don't think so. I think Tyrant Towers is so tall that we've actually gone through the atmosphere." I unstuck my face from the window and turned to her. "We're in space."

6

TURNS OUT
IT IS A THING

The lift stopped.

"Ready to face the Emperor?" I asked.

"I was born to face the Emperor," Holly said, giving me a resolute thumbs up. "Oh no!" Her face fell.

"What?"

"I left my backpack on the spaceship! Can we go back?"

"No way! I'm not spending another minute in this death trap. The spaceship left ages ago anyway. You'll just have to cope with the pants you've got on."

"I'm not turning them inside out if we're still here tomorrow. I'd rather die."

"PING! Welcome to Tyrant Towers, the headquarters of evil itself. Please wipe your feet and prepare to be scanned," said a smooth mechanised voice.

Scanned? We were about to be rumbled. "Where's the scanner?" I yelled. Holly pointed up to a camera in the ceiling. I used the only facility I had at my disposal—slime. I aimed and squirted. The camera was blind. "Scan that, suckers."

"Nice one," Holly said, nodding at me in what almost looked like admiration. But obviously it couldn't have been.

The lift door slid open and we stepped out into a massive carpeted foyer a bit like the lobby of a hotel. There was a check-in desk, a waiting area with comfy sofas and magazines, and framed paintings of the Emperor on the walls looking magnificently evil in the way only a spiky purple blob can. I picked up a leaflet and read: 'Our core values here at Tyrant Towers are present in all we do. Destruction, persecution, supremacy and oppression.' Each 'value' had an accompanying picture, all of which were too nasty to describe here. I put it back down, wincing.

"Oh dear. Oh dear, oh dear. That won't do at all, will it?" Over at the desk, a large spider-like creature with multiple arms and a pinstriped suit on its lozenge-shaped body was addressing a thin, wiry alien like a twisted knot who was standing in front of the desk, visibly shaking.

"I'm s-s-s-sorry, sir! Please don't send me to the Department of Discipline!"

"You were supposed to ensure the new doctors arrived today, Clerk Fifty-One. Don't tell me they're not coming," the spider-like creature said in a sympathetic but hugely disappointed tone.

"I arranged everything just as you asked, sir!" Clerk Fifty-One protested, trembling. "I can only think they must have failed the security scan and been automatically zapped, like most of our other visitors!"

Holly and I exchanged glances. My quick thinking in sliming the camera in the lift had saved our lives. I would remind Holly about that later. Probably quite a few times actually.

"Dear, dear, dear. What am I supposed to tell His Evilness now, hmm?"

"Please forgive me, sir! I promise I'll do better next time!"

"I'm sorry, Clerk Fifty-One. You know the rules. It's the next step on the Consequence Stairway for you, and that's the Department of Discipline I'm afraid. I feel for you, I really do."

"Oh, Mr Pinstripe! No!"

"If it's any consolation, they'll probably just take one of your legs," Mr Pinstripe said consolingly.

"One?"

"One or two."

"But I've only got one or two!"

"Oh yes, I forgot. Well, good luck. Let me know how you get on and keep in touch. Sorry, got to get that." Mr Pinstripe picked up a couple of phones and held one to each ear. "Tyrant Towers, how may we terrify you today?"

We watched Clerk Fifty-One dragging itself miserably across the floor. The thought of whatever awaited it at the Department of Discipline was obviously enough in itself to render it unable to walk.

But it had left us with an opportunity.

"Shall we?" I asked Holly.

"You read my mind," she replied with a wink. "Do you think the Emperor's ill, then?"

"I really hope so."

We approached Clerk Fifty-One as it dragged itself towards a set of double doors.

"Hello there. I wonder if you can help. We've been sent to help out with the Emperor's medical care," Holly said breezily. "It was organised by... Someone Fifty-One?"

It was as though we had inflated a balloon. Fifty-One sprang back to life. I had never seen anyone look so happy, apart from the day Bill finished his to-do list before lunch.

"You're here! You're actually here!" Before we could move, the creature threw its spindly arms around us. "You've saved my life!" it mumbled into Holly's shoulder.

Holly detached it firmly. "That's what we do. Just take us to the Emperor."

"Okay, but you'll need to be signed in, and have your badges, and—oh, I'm so glad you're here! I'm going to live, I'm going to live—aaaoooof."

Fifty-One had fainted—hopefully with joy. We stepped over it and proceeded to the desk.

"Good afternoon," Holly said.

Mr Pinstripe put down the phones he had been speaking into and gave us a warm smile. "How may I help you today? I'm afraid we are only operating at a seventy-six percent level of evil due to the ill health of our esteemed Managing Director Iko Iko Iko, Son of Iko Iko, Grandson of Iko, Emperor of Andromeda Galaxy and Lots of Other Places Too, but we shall try to do our worst for you."

"That's very kind of you." Holly smiled back. "I'm Dr Hol... Holistic, and this is my assistant, Barfbrain."

"That's a nickname, of course," I interrupted. I wasn't about to let Holly get away with giving me a ridiculous name just because she was the first person to speak. "My real name is—"

"Snot Head," Holly said quickly. "That's S N O T, space, H E A D." She spelled it out as Mr Pinstripe typed some letters into a strange keyboard. Two little badges popped out of a drawer.

"So happy that you're here. Would you like to follow me? The Emperor is waiting for you." Mr Pinstripe gave us the badges and stepped out from behind the desk. Seeing all eight limbs, two of them put into service as legs, gave me a shiver and I had to resist the urge to shout for Mary to put a glass over him, slide an envelope underneath and release him into the wild. Actually, he was probably thinking the same thing about me. Instead Holly and I followed him into another lift. This one, thankfully, was on the inside of the building and seemed to operate just like a normal lift. It, too, was made of glass, allowing us a cross-section view of the topmost floors of Tyrant Towers.

As we passed through floor after floor, we could see hundreds of office workers slaving away over computers or sitting around meeting desks pointing at graphs on flip charts and screens showing that evil was definitely on the up.

"I didn't know evil was so well organised," Holly said. "Look, Snot Head. It says that whole floor is just for filing."

"Filing prisoners," Mr Pinstripe informed us. He was right: I could see them trying to get out of the cabinets.

"Oh." Holly looked away quickly.

"Such a shame," Mr Pinstripe said, dabbing at his face with a monogrammed handkerchief. "I feel for them, I do, but rules are rules."

The lift stopped and we entered a plush corridor with an atmosphere of quiet fear. Small, thin creatures almost identical to Clerk Fifty-One flitted past us at intervals carrying covered trays.

Each time they passed us the same exchange

happened.

"Any luck?" Pinstripe would ask.

All of them shook their head.

"Not even a bite? Oh dear. You know what that means, don't you? I'm so sorry. Do recover soon, won't you?"

"Are all those people ill as well?" Jasper asked.

"Ill? Not at all."

"But you told them to get well soon."

"Ah, yes. If they can't tempt the Emperor to eat then sadly they will suffer for their ineptitude. Unfair, I know, but that's the way it is. Ah, here we are."

Pinstripe pushed open a door, revealing a white, sterile-looking room full of surgical equipment. There was a sink in the corner and a row of hooks filled with gowns and masks.

"I'm sure you have what you need, but these were all left by the previous doctors," he explained.

"Previous?"

"The ones who were... who failed to cure the

Emperor. I'm sorry, I was trying to avoid using the word zapped, but you're hardened medical professionals aren't you? I expect you've seen everything."

"Yes, but we haven't seen our own deaths yet, so thank you for your tact," I said grimly.

"You're very welcome. I presume you have experience in extra large mumps crossed with moon stroke?"

I mentally punched the air triumphantly, the concept of my own grisly death at the end of a guard's ray gun instantly forgotten. "So it *is* a thing!"

Holly ignored me. "Naturally. We have extensive experience in that field."

"Thank goodness! His Evilness is getting a little… impatient. Oh, why am I mincing my words again? You're far too professional for me to patronise. Furious. Incandescent. Maniacal. Psychot—"

"I think we get the idea," I interrupted.

"Wonderful. Well, do excuse me, I have a million

things to do and only eight limbs with which to do them. You should find everything you need here, but if there is anything else you require, just press that button and a guard will appear instantly."

"To help us?" Holly asked.

"No, to zap you, I'm afraid. To ask for help is a sign of weakness." Mr Pinstripe held up two of his arms with a helpless smile. "Not my rules."

"Of course not," Holly muttered as the door closed behind him. "All you have to do is implement them."

"I thought he was quite nice," I said. "He really feels for people."

"Yeah, right. Get this on, slugface." Holly thrust a white lab coat at me and slipped one on herself. "Why do you always get us into these ridiculous situations?" she grumbled.

"Me? Anyway, this is perfect. We have direct access to the Emperor himself."

"As his doctors. And he has mumps. I'm just saying right now that if we have to squeeze anything, you're going to squeeze it."

Talking of squeezing, my lab coat was pretty tight. Holly passed me a stethoscope.

"We'd better take these as well," she said, handing me a tray full of equipment which I balanced on my tail.

"What's all this?"

"I don't know, but it looks the part. We'll just have to play along until we hear something useful." Holly smoothed down her lab coat and picked up a small medical bag. She looked really convincing.

I looked like a slug with a giant handkerchief draped over me.

"Wait. Won't he recognise us?"

"Not with these." Holly chucked a surgical mask at me and we popped them on with a twang of elastic. I scrumpled up my eyestalks so they didn't stick out too much. I looked ridiculous—but I was used to that now. At least I didn't look so much like a slug. With any luck the Emperor might even think I was emulating his style.

"How about the tail?" I asked.

"He's probably delirious. He won't notice."

"And if he does?"

Holly pointed to my tray of instruments. "We've got these. He'll be at our mercy."

We headed back out into the plush corridor, got some directions off a terrified Clerk (Thirty-Eight or Thirty-Nine, she didn't stick around long enough for me to remember) and found the doors into His Wobblybottom's private quarters. Very swanky they were too, all floor to ceiling windows, fancy lighting and the obligatory statues of His Yuckiness. Honestly, it really does pay to be an evil alien dictator. If you ever get the chance, go for it.

"This way," a small worm-like creature with glasses told us, wriggling off without giving us a second glance.

"It's her! The one that was talking to the Fluffians on the screen," I whispered to Holly as we walked through a series of anterooms, each one more opulent than the last. There was a soft squeak in my lab coat pocket. I glanced down and saw a small blue ball. "Fluffy!"

"What did you say?"

"Erm, nothing. I was just thinking about the Fluffians. I hope they're okay."

"If you ask me, we're well rid of them. They were only sent to cause trouble. If I never see another one, I'll be happy. You did shake off that one that was riding around on you, didn't you? It looked like it wanted to be your parasite or something."

"Erm, yes, of course. Just button up my pocket for me, would you? I don't want to look unprofessional in front of the Emperor."

Luckily, Holly did as I asked without asking why. Her mind was probably on nobler things, like saving the Earth from alien invasion. For the moment, Fluffy remained undetected. I would have to work out what to do with it later—if there was a later.

Wormy got to a big door and waved a sort of pass thing in the air. The door slid open to reveal a vast, almost empty room. I could just see a massive bed at the other end of it, all canopied and curtained like the sort Henry VIII had slept in. There was a horrible smell and I noticed that there were several guards standing around the edges of the room who all looked slightly revolted and overcome.

"Your new doctors, Your Splendidness," Wormy said in a squeaky voice, bowing low. "You said you wanted to replace the last ones. You know, the ones you zapped for complete incompetence even though they were experts in their field."

Holly and I looked at each other and swallowed nervously.

"May they approach?" Wormy asked.

We were quite near the end of the bed, but not near enough for me to expect what happened next. The Emperor's hand shot out of the bed covers, slapped Wormy around the head and shot back in. It was like a frog catching a fly.

"Of course I want them to approach, you wriggling piece of rancid flesh! They're doctors! I'm ill! Why would I send for doctors if I didn't want them to approach!" The lump on the bed shifted angrily. "Asteroids! I hate being ill! How are my outfits getting on?"

"Your outfits, Your Wondrousness?"

"The ones that I ordered be specially made to disguise my mumps! I've got work to do. Empires to forge. My plans for Earth…"

"That's all under control, Your Graciousness. The outfits and the plans."

"Are they? Are you sure?" The Emperor's hand twitched, ready to strike.

"Yes, yes, Your Bountifulness. I can run through the plans again while you are being examined, if you like."

Holly and I exchanged glances again. We were going to get exactly what we had come in for—the details of the invasion! Things were going so smoothly, it was almost as though they were running along on a trail of well-laid slime. At this rate, Mary and Bill wouldn't even have to know about the proposed invasion and surely that was the best present of all. I imagined their happy smiling faces—

"Well get on with it then!" Wormy snapped at us.

We looked at him blankly.

"The examination?"

"Oh yes." Holly assumed a professional air. "Come along, Snot Head."

"Coming, Dr Ballistic."

"Holistic."

"Whatever."

Cautiously, we drew nearer to the bed. The Emperor lay there in all his blobby purple spikiness. He was like a giant round spiny sea creature, but one that poisoned you for no reason, not a nice one that just floated around looking weird and minding its own business. Luckily, most of him was below a sheet.

Holly set her bag down and opened it up. "How are you feeling today, Your Hugeness? Or can I call you Iko Iko Iko?"

She ducked as the Emperor's hand shot out and missed her head by a hair's breadth.

"I'll take that as a no, shall I?"

"Get on with it!" the Emperor yelled.

"Certainly, Your Heftiness. When did you first notice—"

"The plans! Tell me about the plans!"

Turns out the Emperor wasn't even looking at us. He directed all his attention towards Wormy—or Onefoot, as she seemed to be called—and we were able to listen in as we 'worked'. The trouble was we didn't have a clue what to do.

"Feel his forehead," I suggested. That's what Mary was always doing to us if we claimed we were ill, only it never resulted in anything other than her telling us we were fine and to hurry up or we'd be late for school.

Holly reached out a hand, then recoiled. "I don't want to. You feel his forehead."

"You're the doctor. I'm just the assistant. I haven't qualified in feeling foreheads yet. Plus I haven't got any hands."

Holly scowled at me. With a look of intense

repulsion, she placed a hand on the Emperor's head. Her expression only became more tortured as she made contact.

"The subjects have been brainwashed and released back to Earth. They have taken up their positions at the bartering machines and most have managed to reprogram them to become portals," Onefoot was saying.

"Most?"

"Yes, almost ninety-five percent."

"Zap the other five percent."

"That's a bit difficult from this distance, Your Zealousness."

The Emperor growled. Holly withdrew her hand quickly. "When my army is on Earth, nothing will be difficult," he said menacingly, twisting a ring on his little finger with a large blue and green stone. It looked a lot like a miniature Earth.

There was a pause as Holly and I listened avidly, before remembering we were supposed to be doing an examination.

"Temperature very… high," Holly said quickly. "Or is it low that's the bad one?"

I shrugged. "Either."

"Temperature fluctuating. Make a note of that, Snot Head."

I had absolutely nothing to make notes with, even if I could write. "I shall make a mental note. That's where I keep them. The notes, I mean. In my brain."

Holly glared at me as though all of this was my fault. "Good. Now pass me the… body flange."

"Body flange? Right. Erm…" I leafed through the contents of my tray with my tail. "This one?"

The Emperor and Onefoot were talking again.

"Who knows?" Holly said. "But let's give it a go." I had given her a sort of mirror on a stick; she waved it up and down the Emperor's body, keeping it well above the sheets. "Mmm, very interesting."

"…and the army will ensure total obedience on Earth?" the Emperor was asking.

Onefoot nodded. "Total. They will agree to

anything you say, Your Wondrousness. No need to do things officially when you can control people's minds, after all."

"Whoops!" Holly dropped her implement. It fell into a fold of flesh. She held up her hands, backing away. "Never mind. We've got lots of those."

"Then what's the delay?" the Emperor growled at Onefoot.

"Just some final testing, Your Munificentness, and then the army will be released from the laboratory."

"Laboratory?" I mouthed at Holly. She shrugged back at me, eyebrows raised.

"Haven't you finished yet?" the Emperor barked at us suddenly.

"Nearly." Holly looked about for something else to do.

"Why don't you measure the mump on his head?" I said, flicking her a tape measure from the tray.

Holly gave me a nauseous look. "I think it's time

you did something for a change."

"You're the one with the hands. Come on. Take the tape measure. Get right in close to the Emperor. That's it."

I'm sure Holly probably thought I was being mean making her measure old Blubberboy's lumps and bumps. She really didn't look like she appreciated the opportunity to do something practical to help save the Earth, something she could tell people about and remember all her life.

Well I certainly would remember this moment all my life. Watching Holly examining the Emperor of Andromeda's mump was the most revolting thing I have ever had to do in my whole life, and I've bathed in slime.

"It's… five centimetres high," Holly said in a strangled voice.

"And how many centimetres around?" I asked brightly. Just for the sake of thoroughness, you understand.

"I'm done!" Holly yelped, throwing the tape

measure at me and squirming away from the bed.

"You didn't collect a sample of the fluid," I said.

"I hate you."

I won't tell you what happened next, because I'm nice like that. All you need to know is that eventually Holly had a pocket full of the Emperor's mump juice. Luckily it was in a bottle. It looked and smelled like the worst perfume ever.

"Now tell me your diagnosis and get out," the Emperor grunted.

Holly cleared her throat. "You have extra large mumps and moon stroke."

"I knew that! Useless pair! Zap them, guards!"

"Wait!" Holly said quickly. "You also have a very severe case of egotistical dictatormania."

"Ego what? What's that?"

"Nothing to be concerned about. You just need to rest."

"That's right. Stay in bed," I added. "Relax. Stop getting involved in everything. There's no I in team, you know. Let Onefoot take the strain for a bit.

You're stressed, and that's stopping you from getting better."

"Colouring in is very therapeutic," Holly added. "We'll get you some colouring books. What are your interests?"

"Death and destruction!" the Emperor growled.

"Fine. We'll see what we can do."

Holly picked up her bag. I grabbed the tray. It was time to leave while we were still unrecognised and unzapped. We hurried to the door.

"Wait!" the Emperor bellowed.

We had been so close to escaping. We turned, waiting, ready for the inevitable zapping. I wondered if my slime could protect us, or if I could zap the guards before they got us. Trouble was, there were so many of them. I tensed up and closed my eyes, waiting for the Emperor's command.

"Colouring books, you say? Do you have any with… unicorns in?"

"Unicorns?" I blurted out incredulously, opening my eyes. Holly stood on my tail. "Ow!"

"I like unicorns," the Emperor snapped.

"Of course, Your Evilness," Holly said, bowing. "We will get that to you as soon as possible. Thank you for your time. Thank you. Goodbye."

We backed away and were accompanied out by Onefoot.

"Well, congratulations," she said as the door slid shut behind us. "You didn't get zapped after all. But I hope for your sake you've got a unicorn colouring book ready, or prepare to have your flesh singed."

"Of course," Holly said, nodding professionally. "We'll need some time. Only the best for the Emperor."

Onefoot marched us back to the corridor. "You have thirty zerkoids," she said, giving us a threatening glare and slamming the door.

7

TURNS OUT HOLLY
CAN'T SPELL UNICORN

"Zerkoids?" I asked Holly.

"Must be a unit of time," Holly said. "But how long? It could be a second or a day."

"Knowing the Emperor, it's the first one. Better prepare to be zapped then. There's no chance of getting a unicorn colouring book. Great idea of yours, Holly. Hey, where are you going?"

I followed Holly to the medical room, where she rummaged around the supplies and managed to find some scraps of paper and thick pens. "Get drawing."

"What? Why me?"

"I'm going to find out where the laboratory is and take a look at this weird army the Emperor's on about."

"Hang on—no! *I'm* going to find out where the laboratory is. You can sit and draw stupid unicorns for old Blubberface."

"No way!"

We glared at each other.

Holly sighed. "Fine. Half each and we'll both go."

"You're forgetting something," I told her, holding up my tail to demonstrate my lack of fingers.

Holly poked me with a pencil. I opened my mouth to object and she shoved the pencil in it. "Draw."

Five minutes later we had a stack of drawings which would have made my art teacher weep, and not with joy at my undiscovered artistic genius. I blame the pens. They had finger holes and possibly doubled as musical instruments. Leonardo da Vinci would have struggled. And he had fingers.

Holly looked through our attempts. "That one's not too bad," she said, holding up a scribble.

"That was me trying to get the pen to work. But who cares? Shove it in."

Holly found a big clip to hold the pages together. "Look, I've made a cover," she said, putting it at the front.

"You've missed out the I," I told her.

"Have I? Like you say, who cares? Right, let's find that lab!"

We rushed towards the door just as it opened. Onefoot stood in our way. "Thirty zerkoids," she squeaked delightedly. "Time to show the Emperor you can cure him, or it's zappy zappy time."

"You actually like the zapping stuff, don't you?" I said.

"It's part of my job description."

"That's what you all say," Holly muttered darkly.

Onefoot wriggled to the table and picked up the wad of clipped sheets, the result of a fusion of two brilliantly creative minds focused on saving humanity. "What's an Uncorn?"

"It's not for you, it's for the Emperor," Holly said

hotly. "And you are delaying his treatment."

"Fair enough," Onefoot smirked. "Far be it from me to hold up your imminent deaths."

We followed Onefoot back to the Emperor's chambers with heavy hearts. Everything rested on our artistic talents.

"If I'd known being good at drawing would save the Earth from alien invasion, I'd have tried harder in art lessons," I muttered to Holly. Ironically, I was quite good at doodling spaceships and aliens. I comforted myself with the thought that even the professionals struggled with a horse.

We bowed and scraped our way towards the Emperor's bed. His giant mumps looked worse than ever, especially the massive one on his head which seemed to have been aggravated by its recent inspection by Doctor Holistic. Shame.

"Well?" he demanded, trying to sit up and collapsing back onto about fifty pillows.

"As prescribed, here is your colouring book, Your Evilness," Holly said, proffering the artistic abomination.

The Emperor's frog-tongue-like hand whipped out and snatched it from her. "The Uncorn Colouring Book," he read.

"It's a type of unicorn."

"I wanted actual unicorns!" the Emperor bellowed, throwing the book across the room.

Holly dived for it and pressed it back into his hand. "They are unicorns, I promise," she said. "Look. There's a horn. There's some hooves. And that's the eye."

The Emperor grudgingly looked through some pages. "Unicorns are supposed to be beautiful."

"These are realistic unicorns. Not all beauty is on the outside, Your Corpulentness. Some people look absolutely hideous, but on the inside—"

"What's this?" the Emperor yelled, prodding at one of the pictures. "This isn't a unicorn! It's big and slimy. This is a giant slug. A slug with a horn. It's a unislug!"

Holly shot me a look sharper than any horn.

Whoops. I hadn't been thinking when I'd done that one. "You've drawn a self-portrait, you idiot!" she hissed.

"What? I haven't got a unicorn horn," I pointed out.

"You will have when I've driven this felt tip pen through your head!"

This time the Emperor managed to sit up. "A giant slug. I've seen one of them before." His nasty little eyes widened as he looked at me properly for the first time. "It's him! The Slime Prince of Gloop! Zap him, zap him, zap him!" he yelled, his purple spines wobbling with fury.

The guards, who had been yawning as usual, started shaking themselves awake. Holly and I scrambled madly towards the door. Onefoot stood in the way, smiling nastily.

"Hop on," I ordered Holly.

"No way! I'm not riding on you—hey!"

I scooped her up with my tail and plonked her on my back. With a squirt of slime, we skidded out of the door, right over the top of the tiny Onefoot.

"Is she dead?" Holly asked.

I swivelled my eyes around. "No."

"Bother. To the lift!"

The lift stood open at the end of the corridor. The guards were chasing us and from the sound of it they weren't far behind. Purple bolts of light shot past us and zapped off the walls.

"Giddy up! Faster, faster!" Holly yelled, slapping me on the flanks.

We zoomed into the lift with a squelch.

"What floor? What floor?" Holly muttered, scanning the multiple columns of buttons.

"Just shut the door!" I shouted, dodging to the left as a massive shot from a guard's laser narrowly missed me. "I'm a bigger target than you!"

The door slid shut, blocking a hail of laser fire. Holly and I collapsed against the wall. I checked on Fluffy. It was still in my pocket, its little face looking all excited at the mayhem.

"Giddy up?" I repeated, turning on Holly.

"You deserved it, unislug."

Fair enough. It had been my terrible drawing that had given us away. Although the Emperor had recognised it as me so actually it must have been pretty good. "So where are we going?" I asked, getting my breath back.

Holly's eyes sparkled. "Laboratories, of course. It's clearly labelled right here. And if the guards are as thick as the Emperor's last lot, they'll take a while to track us down. They'll probably assume we're making a run for it, not sticking around to cause more mayhem. This is our chance."

It really was. The momentous nature of what we were doing seemed to dawn on both of us. We fell silent, getting our breath back as the lift descended. We were a team now, working together with almost telepathic ease.

"Thanks for coming with me, Hols," I said quietly.

Holly shook her head. "No, thanks for coming with *me*."

What was she on about? "Hang on, this is my mission. You're just helping."

"No, you're helping *me*. You didn't think you were in charge, did you? Aw, that's so sweet."

"Stop it! You've never been in charge! This is all about me!—Never mind, we're here."

We were in a maze of long white corridors with multiple doors leading off them. Several people moved from room to room wearing white coats and carrying clipboards. They spoke in hushed, serious voices and used lots of bizarre scientific words, like 'string theory' and 'quark'. Luckily, we were still wearing our white coats too and they accepted our presence without comment, even if we didn't join in with the quark comments. The atmosphere was quiet yet busy; gentle beeping, whirring and clicking noises complemented the background hum of serious scientific endeavour. Or making lots of evil stuff.

"I don't know about you, but I'm finding it a teensy bit worrying that the army is kept in a laboratory," Holly said, as we hurried round another corner and followed the arrows pointing to 'Main Lab'. "What do you think they are? Robots?

Cyborgs? Some sort of hideous genetic experiments?"

"If they come from the Emperor's mind, then they'll definitely be hideous," I said with a shiver. What would we find? And, more importantly, what could we do to stop them? "Left here," I added as we turned into yet another white corridor.

Holly stopped dead. "Oh my god!"

"What? Is it a hideous genetic experiment?"

"No, it's—it's—oh!"

Holly staggered back in a half-faint. I caught her with my tail and pushed her back upright as Harry Handsome swaggered down the corridor towards us, pushing his floppy fringe out of his eyes with a casual sweep of his hand.

"Harry was supposed to catch me, not you!" Holly hissed, pushing me away. "Hi Harry!" she added in a completely different voice. "I loved your concert the other day. And you couldn't even tell you were using a backing track—it really sounded like you were playing the guitar all by yourself."

I ignored her. "Doing the Emperor's dirty work,

are you? Well, you're not hypnotising us."

Harry looked at us curiously. His floppy fringe fell back into his eyes. "Hello. Are you my friends?"

"No, we are not your friends! As if! Watch out Holly, he's trying to hypnotise you again," I warned her.

"Ooh, what's that?" Harry said, pointing at the wall with dopey fascination.

"A light switch? Like the one that's just switched off in your head? Come on, Hols, let's go before he blabs to the Emperor."

Harry stopped pointing at the light switch and looked at me with a puzzled expression. "Who's the Emperor? Is he my friend?"

"Oh, how adorable—I think he's got concussion!" Holly squealed. "We can take him home with us and nurse him back to health!"

"Concussion? What from? Don't be daft! He's not ill, he's just trying to play with your mind, like he did with all those other fans."

"Who's that?" Harry said, pointing at his face on

Holly's t-shirt. "Can I be your friend too?" he asked his own image.

"You're right, he is ill," I agreed. "He doesn't even recognise himself, and that's the person he looks at more than anybody." There was no choice. "We'd better take him with us before he regains his sanity and realises what we're up to."

Holly linked her arm with Harry's. "Don't worry, I'm a doctor," she told him happily.

This was getting weirder and weirder, but I couldn't think of an alternative and Holly didn't want to. We had to carry on and complete our mission with Happy Harry in tow. The corridor turned again and this time there was a big set of doors at the end with 'LABORATORY' written over them in flashing green letters.

"Ooh, pretty!" Harry said in a sing-song voice.

"He's so cute like this," Holly cooed.

As we stood there wondering what to do, a head poked out of the door and a spiky-haired woman with lilac-coloured skin stared at us through thick goggles that magnified her eyes.

"You've found him! Praise the Empire. Don't just stand there. Bring him in, quickly. If news of this gets out, the Emperor will have us all zapped. Well, come on!"

"Yes, professor," I said quickly.

She held the door open for us and we took Harry into the lab. It was a huge white room lined with worktops, all full of scientific equipment. But it was also full of something else. The army. A work of pure evil genius, and my ultimate nightmare.

"Harry Handsomes!" I gasped. "Hundreds of them!"

8

TURNS OUT ONE HARRY
IS NEVER ENOUGH

"One hundred, to be precise. Beautiful, aren't they?" the woman said proudly. The label on her lab coat said she was Professor Placebo. "This batch is straight out of the cloning machine. A little basic at the moment, but they won't be once they've progressed to the Intelligence Room to be refined. Not too much, mind you. We're trying to match the original as closely as possible."

It was a scene that sent a stab of horror into my heart. Rows upon rows of Harry Handsomes, all wearing his trademark white t-shirt, jeans and jacket. All with the exact same number of hairs falling across their silly, smiling faces.

"Will you be my friend?" our Harry asked, approaching one of the other Harrys. The other one stared round uncomprehending.

"Your escapee appears to have developed too early," the professor said. "It's showing signs of having a mind of its own. That won't do at all. I'll have to incinerate it."

"What? No!" Holly yelped, grabbing hold of the Harry.

"Let go of it!" the professor said sternly. She eyed us more keenly. "Who are you? How did you get past security?"

"The Emperor knows we're here," I said quickly. Which was true. "We're... er... clone disposal experts." Which was not true. Or maybe it was. I mean, who else was there who knew anything about the disposal of clones? We could well be the experts with zero knowledge.

The professor blinked. "I wasn't expecting you. I didn't even know this one had malfunctioned until it wandered off five minutes ago."

"Ah, yes, well, as experts in the field, we know that for every batch of clones, there's usually one that goes wrong. So we routinely visit sites where cloning is taking place in order to offer our services." I glanced at Holly, who nodded at my impressive off-the-cuff improvisation.

"I see." The professor still sounded as though she didn't believe our made-up-on-the-spot story. Which was no doubt why she was a professor in the first place. "And you are called…?"

"Clone Sweet Clone. Clone disposal and rehabilitation." I was on *fire*.

"I don't want this clone rehabilitated. I want him disposed of. And I have a perfectly good incinerator myself. How much are you charging for this 'service'?"

I didn't like the way she was putting invisible speech marks around the word 'service'. "Ah, well that's the beauty of our system. We reuse the clone parts and make a profit that way, so we don't charge you, the client, anything at all."

Holly leaned in. "And we promise not to tell the Emperor that your experimentations have gone a little... pear-shaped."

The professor bristled, her eyes seeming to grow even bigger behind her goggles. "Very well," she said finally. "One in every batch, you say?"

"That's the statistics talking, not me."

"I suppose I'd better check the other batches, then. Wait here. I may have more to give you." She bustled off through another door.

"Can I design the logo?" Holly asked.

"What?"

"For Clone Sweet Clone."

"No! I've seen your attempts at unicorns. Or uncorns, as you spell them. This isn't even a real company, remember?" I added as Holly looked disappointed.

"What are these?" Harry said, holding up his fingers and wriggling them. The other Harrys looked on blankly.

"They're called fingers, Harry," Holly explained

patiently. "And these are your hands." She turned to me. "I can't believe it. I thought the Emperor was mean and horrible, but he's going to give Earth the best present of all—more Harrys!"

"Remember what Harry does? He hypnotises people! We're going to become a nation of weak-brained idiots who do everything the Emperor says. Some of us already are," I added pointedly. "Don't you see, Holly? He doesn't need to invade anymore because he'll command the Harrys and the Harrys will command us! He may as well have a giant remote control pointed at the Earth."

Holly slumped. "Alright, alright. Couldn't you let me just enjoy the idea for one minute? So what now?"

"We've got two choices," I said, starting to count them on my fingers, remembering I didn't have any and using Harry's instead. At least he would learn one use for them. "One: destroy all the Harrys."

"No! They're innocent, Jasper. We can't do that."

"Or two, destroy the portals."

"But that could be dangerous for the people who are working at them at Asbi's. They're innocent too."

"You're right. Okay then, three," I said, grabbing another of Harry's fingers. He didn't seem to mind. "We need to destroy the way the portals work."

Holly waggled her eyebrows furiously at me and I realised she was trying to tell me that Professor Placebo was standing behind me listening to every word I said.

I dropped Harry's hand. "Ah, professor. I was just saying that defective clones could destroy the way the portals work, if we aren't careful."

The professor narrowed her eyes. "You seem to know a lot about Operation Heartthrob."

"Is that what it's called? I mean, oh yes. I always do my research."

"I suppose that's to be commended. Well, a defective clone would still pass through the portal, but could misinterpret instructions the other end, so it's better to weed them out and destroy them at an early stage."

"Of course," I agreed.

"And I expect, as the Emperor's top scientist, it will be you who opens the portals?" Holly asked.

"That's very kind of you to say so, but the Emperor likes to control everything himself. In fact, he has had the button embedded into a special ring with a jewel that looks like the Earth, which he wears on his little finger. Always the one for the grand statement."

"Really? I mean, of course."

Holly and I exchanged glances. The ring on his finger! We began sidling towards the door.

"Right. We'll be off then," I said cheerfully. "With the defective clone. Thank you for doing business with Clone Sweet Clone."

"Logo in development," Holly added.

"Wait a minute!" The professor opened the other door and ushered in three more Harrys. "These are defective too."

"Hello. Will you be my friend?" all three Harrys said in unison.

"Oh no," I groaned.

Holly's eyes lit up. "Lovely. We'll take them. Thank you *so* much."

"Don't forget to use us again. Clone Sweet Clone at your service," I said, smiling until we had taken the four Harrys out of the lab and back into the corridor, where my smile turned into a grimace. "Four of them?" I wailed. "Could this get any worse?"

"You're my best friend," the nearest Harry said, putting his arms around me.

Yes, it could.

"Well you're not mine," I said, detaching him firmly. The Harry's eyes filled with tears.

"Don't say that!" Holly snapped. "He's still being trained—it'll affect his whole outlook on life. Hang on, that gives me an idea. We'll need an empty lab, a bit of time, and these four Harrys."

We hurried back down the corridor, peering through porthole-shaped windows into mysterious laboratories. In one, small scientists were balancing large white cubes on top of each other which lit up when they connected. In another, purple-faced scientists a bit like Professor Placebo were bouncing rays of light off the walls as they walked around on a huge map.

"Planning his next invasion," I muttered to Holly, but she was ahead of me. In the corridor, I mean, not in her thought process, although knowing her she was probably ahead of me in that area as well.

"Look in here," she called, waving me over.

I slid towards her, which was getting difficult as all the Harrys kept trying to hold on to me and tell me how much they loved me.

"They've got attached to you really quickly, haven't they?" Holly marvelled.

"Tell me about it," I said, wincing. "What's in there, then?"

"Looks like the Emperor's new clothes."

I peered in through the small round window. Zap! A pulse of purple light shot over my shoulder and past Holly's ear.

"Surrender in the name of Iko Iko Iko, Son of Iko

Iko, Grandson of—oh forget it, just surrender, intruder scum!" screamed the voice of a guard.

"In here," I said, throwing open the door. Holly and I shoved the Harrys through and she slammed the door after us.

We were faced with a line of hideous draping costumes hung over metal Emperor-shaped frames like crude shop window mannequins. The fabrics were patterned with what looked like exploding planets—or exploding people. I tried not to look at the details too hard. Maybe that passed for high fashion around here if you were a giant purple spiky blob.

"What are you doing, Jasper? Under this counter quick!" Holly called.

I crawled under the counter, finding myself between two Harrys who hugged me enthusiastically.

"Can't I just stay outside and be zapped instead?" I asked.

"Speak for yourself. I could stay here forever." Holly's grin disappeared. "Shh! They're coming in."

We heard the door fly open and the thud of footsteps as the guards ran into the lab.

"Are they our friends?" the Harry next to me asked hopefully.

"No," I hissed. "And we won't be either if you don't shut up."

We stayed very still and listened to the guards' voices as they clomped around the lab.

"No one here, mate."

"You sure? What's that then?"

"New clobber for the Emperor to cover up his mumps so he can go to all those intergalactic meeting thingies and take over more galaxies."

"Hee hee hee. More zapping for us. Here, I hope we don't catch them mumps off him."

"How do you know if you have?"

"You get great big lumps all over you, don't you? Hang on, I think you've got one already."

"What? Where?"

"In the middle of your face. My mistake, it's your nose."

"Are you saying I've got a big nose?"

"Nah, course not. Everyone else is though."

"What? Right, you're paying for that!"

Thud! Pow! It sounded like the two guards were fighting amongst themselves. It was good to hear.

Suddenly I had a eureka moment. It was either the best idea I'd ever had, or the worst. Sometimes you could only judge these things once they were over. "I think I've got an idea."

"Does it hurt?" Harry Two asked, looking concerned.

"Wait a minute, I never got to tell you about my idea," Holly said.

"Go on then." My idea was so good it could wait another minute, as long as it *was* only a minute.

We both winced as we heard the sound of one of the guards hitting the floor.

"I was thinking," Holly continued, "that maybe I could train the Harrys to be good instead of evil, and then smuggle them back into the cloning lab to teach the others."

"That's brilliant! The Emperor could release nice

Harrys instead of nasty ones. And that fits in perfectly with my idea. How do you feel about splitting up for a bit?"

Holly gave me a look. "I've got four Harry Handsomes. Of course I want to get rid of you for a bit."

"Fine. I'll buy you some time. How much do you think you need?"

Holly considered. "As much as you can get. But I'll need to know when the clone invasion is imminent so I can release the Harrys back into the cloning lab and give them time to affect the others."

"I'll do what I can. Or maybe I'll be able to get the ring so we won't have to."

"Alright, but say goodbye properly to the Harrys. They're really going to miss you."

I ignored her request and crawled out of the cabinet. The guards had managed to knock each other out. I didn't understand how that was possible, but I was glad it was. They couldn't hear the Harrys crying at my sudden departure, plus it gave me time

to choose my outfit. From now on, I wasn't Jasper Clarkson, secret Slime King of Gloop any longer. I was Emperor Iko Iko Iko, Son of Iko Iko, Grandson of... never mind. I was the evil Emperor of Andromeda.

I popped Fluffy down on the floor for some exercise and began to choose my outfit.

It was time to do things *my* way.

9

TURNS OUT EVERYONE'S GOT A GIANT PURPLE ALIEN DICTATOR INSIDE THEM

So, here we are. I'm sitting at this massive desk, at the top of the most impressive building on the planet, yelling at the head of my vast military resources and giving the command to invade Earth.

Can I be hearing this right? I hear you asking yourselves. Has our hero finally lost it? Has he become so corrupted by his new powers that he can't remember why he was here in the first place?

In a way, yes.

The first few days were amazing. First I had to force my sluggy body into one of the metal Emperor-shaped frames that displayed his new clothing. That wasn't easy, although it helped being a slug as I was more slippery and flexible than I would have been if human. I just about got myself into it and by folding my eyestalks I was able to line up my eyes with the eyeholes. The fabric draped down to the floor and covered my tail. By the time the guards had recovered from their fight I was standing over them demanding to be escorted to my throne room—or 'office' as I found out it was called.

I told them old Blubberface in the bedroom was a hideous imposter, planted there by some rogue doctors who had recently gone on the run. I think they were quite keen to believe it. The real Emperor (or the fake Emperor, as I officially renamed him) was foul and ugly. I was clean-smelling—well, relatively—and hidden under a sheet. Of course they preferred me.

Ruling Andromeda was absolutely nothing like ruling Gloop. On Gloop, my duties consisted of opening fetes (yawn), visiting the slime mines (delightful—not), kissing babies (yuck) and posing for postage stamps (pretty dull once you've got over the novelty of licking your own head). On AndroSphere, it was a bit different.

"What would Your Fabulousness like for breakfast?" was the first thing I heard every morning from one of the many clerks (I gave up trying to tell them apart) when I woke up in my circular triple-sprung bed. The Emperor was locked in the best bedroom—my orders—but luckily the second best bedroom was fit for a ten-star hotel.

"Erm, er, let me think. Today I would like chocolate sponge with syrup and marshmallows."

"Chocolate bonge with what, Your Awesomeness?"

"Or the nearest equivalent. And double check that outrageous imposter who claimed he was the real Emperor is still locked in my bedroom!"

"Clerk Ninety-Nine will carry out your orders immediately, Your Uniqueness."

After my bespoke breakfast, I would lie around on giant pillows being entertained by various members of staff who were commanded to distract me from my illness. To stay in character, it was

necessary to treat every attempt with total disdain, even if I really liked them. At first, I had to fight to suppress my natural enthusiasm, but after a while it got easier each day to be rude. I guess being horrible just takes a bit of practice.

The rest of the day was spent stuffing my face with lunch, followed by more lying around, followed by a bit more face-stuffing. Officially I was 'recuperating' from my illness. It was great. Especially the food. On Gloop, everything had been made of slime. Unofficially I was trying to buy Holly some time. How much, I didn't know. How long did it take to train the clones of a pop star to be a force for good and be able to train other clones to be the same? I had the ring, which I had commanded be ripped off the evil usurper's hand (I hope it hurt) and wore it on a chain around my neck, but I didn't know if the Emperor had another way of opening the portals, or whether he had already given a command to his underlings to release them at a certain time. I could be found out at any moment.

All I could do was keep the deception going as long as I could. My only comfort was that Fluffy was still with me, clinging to my tail and occasionally zooming up to look out of an eyehole. It helped me to feel less alone.

Unfortunately I was only able to hold off enquiries about the invasion plans for so long. Eventually I began to receive requests for meetings from General Shootemdown, a character I wasn't very keen to meet just on the basis of hearing their name. My lack of aggression towards neighbouring galaxies was looking suspicious, however, and so eventually I had to give in and asked to be helped to my office.

The general stood in front of me. It was hard to focus on her scarred, battle-worn face with her huge weaponised arms taking up most of the bulk of her body.

"The clones are ready, Your Brilliantness. All that remains is for you to open the portals."

"Right. Right."

"Which you haven't done yet." The general was looking suspiciously at the ring, which hung from a chain around my neck.

"I have been ill, you know!" I snapped. "I don't just wear this sheet for fun—I'm hideous under here." I shifted around inside the framework of the mannequin. It was hot and sweaty in here and made me irritable. On the other hand, it was very useful for channelling those grouchy vibes.

"Of course you are, Your Unsightliness." The general gave a little bow of apology. "It's just that, you did say that you would open the portals as soon as possible. You were very keen." She narrowed her eyes. "And now you're not."

I paced up and down to buy some time to think. It was difficult with only one foot and draped in an enormous cloth patterned with exploding enemies. The eyeholes kept shifting around when I moved. I bumped into a wall and turned round.

"As it happens," I said imperiously. "I have changed my mind."

"What!" General Shootemdown nearly fell over, just like one of her legendary victims.

"Yes, I've decided not to invade Earth after all. I'm like that, aren't I? Always changing my mind. Typical villain."

"No, Your Constancy. You never change your mind. You've always wanted to take over Earth. Are you sure your illness hasn't affected you?"

"Are you saying I've gone doolally? Because if you are…" I let my voice trail away. Mainly because I couldn't think of anything to say. She might expect me to carry out any threat I suggested.

"Not at all, Your Saneness. But you've always wanted Earth. You said it would be the jewel in your collection. And that human beings were stupid and deserved all they got."

"Now that's not true!" I blurted out hotly. "Human beings are brilliant."

General Shootemdown nearly fell over again. She staggered against the wall and stared at me in disbelief. I saw her weaponised arms twitch.

"No, no! Brilliantly stupid, I mean." I was sweating like mad under the costume. Was there no way out of this?

"Perhaps," the general said, standing upright again and moving towards me slowly and purposefully, "I should give the command to activate the portals myself. As you are so very, *very* sick."

"No! I hate Earth, I really do! I'll open the portals. But... but first..." I tried to think of something to delay the inevitable. Anything. "I want to interrogate the criminal who has been impersonating me. We... we need to make sure he— or she—hasn't changed any of the plans. Well don't just stand there! Lead me to him. My eyeholes are slipping."

"Yes, Your Forcefulness."

Sighing with frustration and trying not to panic, I left the huge office accompanied by General Shootemdown and a small team of armed guards, declining the offer of being carried on the Emperor's usual hammock. It was bad enough trying to keep myself covered while I was on the ground. We entered the Emperor's private lift. It was very swish with a chandelier, soft cushions and a drinks cabinet, but I didn't have time to dwell on luxuries. How much longer did Holly need? I had no way of knowing. All I could do was play for time and make my interview with the Emperor last as long as possible. Well, that might not be too hard. I certainly had a lot to say to him, the evil, greedy, galaxy-conquering maniac. It was time to have it out with Mr Blobbychops once and for all. The power was on my side now and I would make him pay for everything he had done, the ugly, slimy, despicable—

Jasper!

…deluded, self-important, deranged…

Jasper!

…crazy, blubber-bottomed…

Jasper, remember who you are!

"What? Who is that?"

Remember your families, on Earth and on Gloop. Remember kindness, tolerance and tinned tuna.

"Eh?"

"Are you alright, Your Despicableness?" General Shootemdown asked brusquely.

We were descending. The general was fixing me a cocktail. There seemed to be a voice saying my name coming out of the walls.

"I'm fine. It's because I've been ill," I gabbled.

"Should I fetch a doctor, Your Confusedness?"

"No! In fact, how dare you stray outside your job description and take interest in my welfare like this! I should have you zapped."

The general looked reassured at my outburst. The lift opened and we were in the Emperor's private apartments. I could hear cries of rage coming from the bedroom. But I could also still hear the strange voice. It seemed to be somewhere in the ceiling this time, or maybe the walls.

Jasper, be true to yourself.

"I know what you are!" I said triumphantly. "The

voice of my conscience!"

"I don't think so, Your Deludedness."

"Not you!" I barked at the general. "The voice in the walls."

The general was looking at me with a very odd expression. I was at risk of blowing my cover. I bit back any more comments about disembodied voices and slid along under my sheet.

"Unlock the door," I commanded. "Guards, be ready but don't fire. Remember, this is an intruder. He may claim to be me. Ignore him. I'm the real Emperor, not him." I realised this was just the sort of thing a fake Emperor would say, but there was no way round it.

The general opened the door and we entered. There was a roar of fury from the bed at the other end of the room. Onefoot, whom I had forgotten was locked in there as well, scurried up to us, her glasses askew and sweat pouring down her little wormy face.

"Please! Let me out! I can't stand another minute in here!" she pleaded, choking. It was smelling pretty disgusting in there.

"Can we zap them both? Can we?" the guards asked, pointing their lasers at Onefoot and the Emperor who was struggling to get out of his bed and failing, badly.

"The Emperor will be interrogating the usurper. But not this one." General Shootemdown raised her gun-arm and pointed it at Onefoot. "Prepare to die, you measly little traitor."

"Hang on, hang on. You can't just kill her," I said.

The general turned to me, her gun still pointed at Onefoot who was squirming in terror.

"Because. She's little. And wormy. She's like a little worm. And it wasn't really her fault. She—"

"Oh, just zap the creepy little weirdo!" the Emperor yelled out.

The general, the guards and Onefoot all looked at the Emperor. Then they looked at me.

"I'm the real Emperor!" I said desperately. "But you can't zap her." It was then that I uttered the fatal word that would be my downfall. I blame Mary and

Bill. They had taught me to be polite since the day they had started fostering me, and it was very hard to resist ten years of rigorous training. How could they have known that teaching me good manners would lead to my doom? "Please?" I asked.

Onefoot pointed at me and started jumping up and down. "False Emperor! False Emperor!" she squeaked. Well there's gratitude for you.

The laser guns that had been aimed at the Emperor were now aimed at me. I shrunk away inside my disguise but there was nowhere to go.

"Well, well, well," General Shootemdown said, circling me with her gun-shaped arms pointing and ready to fire. A slow smile was spreading across her face. "So you're the fake Emperor, not him? I should have realised." She pointed a gun at my chest. I closed my eyes, bracing myself, and heard a metallic snap as the chain around my neck broke. I opened my eyes in time to see the ring being tossed to a guard, who caught it and chucked it to the Emperor.

"Of course he's the fake Emperor, you brain-dead trigger-happy pea-brain!" the Emperor yelled. "I've never said the word please in my life! Well, I have now but that doesn't count, it was only to illustrate a point. Bring him to me!"

The guards herded me at gunpoint to the foot of the bed. I tried to keep my nerve and look the Emperor straight in the eye, but it was difficult as my left eye hole was now halfway down my face and my tail was sticking out due to it shaking so much. My only comfort was that the Emperor looked as ill as ever. The giant mump on his head was bright red and inflamed. Our 'treatment' had only made things worse. Good.

"Unmask the imposter," the Emperor commanded, sliding the ring back onto his stubby finger.

With a flourish worthy of a TV surprise home makeover show, General Shootemdown whisked off my disguise and I was displayed in all my slimy sluginess. There was a collective gasp, which I thought was a bit rich considering the state of the Emperor.

"Some would say your shape is its own punishment," the Emperor said, looking down at me from his pile of pillows.

"Ah, well that's where you're wrong. Being a slug is great," I lied. "This is a lifestyle choice actually."

"Of course it is. I expect your royal parents are thrilled—they always did lack ambition. Now they have a son to match their own pathetic dreams."

I flicked my tail with anger. "At least they never dreamed about taking over Earth. No one wants a big self-obsessed blob in charge."

"For a prince, you have a very poor understanding of politics, don't you? It's not about what people want. People aren't important." He said the word 'people' like it was a contagious disease. "Who cares about people? It's about what I want. And *I* want Earth."

"It's not yours to take!" I shouted.

Everything went green. For a moment I thought it was rage, like the red mist you read about in books that comes down when people get angry and makes them do things they wouldn't normally do. Was I about to make a run for it, dodge past a hail of laser fire and dive for the door as it began to close, rolling under it and only pausing to offer a parting salute (the rude kind), to the accompaniment of an exciting orchestral soundtrack?

No. Turns out the Emperor's mump had burst.

The green mist was actually something completely disgusting that spurted out and covered us all. This was good news for me—although I would have preferred the good news to be delivered in a slightly nicer, less pus-like way—as it created confusion. Everyone yelped with horror. I dived under General Shootemdown's lethal limbs and skidded to the door. No need for slime—there was plenty of stuff to skid on already. I would have to remember to wash my foot later.

I threw myself at the door which slid open. At last! Freedom! I breathed a sluggy sigh of relief, and came face to face with Mr Pinstripe.

He gave me a polite spidery smile. "I'm dreadfully sorry to be the bearer of bad news, but apparently I have to take you to prison."

I was about to dodge past him, hopefully flattening him on the way, but I felt the end of General Shootemdown's finger gun in one ear and the breath of an armed guard in the other.

"Is it a nice prison with table tennis and a giant screen?" I asked hopefully.

Mr Pinstripe looked as though he was trying to be cheerful for my sake. "Captivon? I'm afraid not. It's a horrible prison planet with no way of escape and giant three-headed robotic guards. But I'm sure you'll settle in eventually. Most prisoners do. Or they die. Either way, you get used to it."

I sighed. "Sounds great."

"Wait!" the Emperor bellowed.

I spun round. Was he about to offer me a last minute reprieve? It would be just like a film where the hero was saved at the very last minute as the villain realised what a complete numpty he had been. I wondered how the Emperor would phrase his surrender speech.

"I want to open the portals in front of you, to see the hope die in your eyes."

"No!" I yelled, at the same time as the Emperor pressed his ring. A distant siren sounded from somewhere far below and the hope died in my eyes. I turned away so the Emperor couldn't see.

"We'll travel by spacelift," Pinstripe said, scuttling ahead officiously as the guards prodded me forward with their weapons.

"My favourite mode of transport," I muttered bitterly. "You don't have to do this, Mr Pinstripe."

"I know," Pinstripe said with a tone of polite sorrow. "But orders are orders."

My stomach churned in anticipation as we proceeded grimly to the private lift. General Shootemdown raised a weapon in farewell. Onefoot stuck her tongue out. Behind me, I heard the Emperor's triumphant laugh. In silence, we moved to the internal lift and finally to the external lift which would go into space. They were really obsessed with lifts in this place.

Mr Pinstripe and two guards squeezed in with me. I squished myself into the corner and stared out into the heavily starred sky as we zoomed off. I had failed. I hadn't even been able to warn Holly. Everything now rested on her having managed to reprogram the Harry clones, and we didn't even know if that would work or what effect it would have. Had I even bought her enough time? My heart sank even further as I remembered the adoption party. Had we missed it? But then I guessed a party didn't matter that much anymore if Earth was about to be taken over by a big spiky blob. If only I had waited for Flarp, but I had stupidly decided that Holly and I could do this on our own. Big mistake.

Remember, you are not alone.

"Oh, go away," I said to the voice in the ceiling.

"I'm afraid that's not possible, Mr Slug," Pinstripe said with a gracious smile. "We have to accompany you to your cell. But don't worry, we'll be going away after that, for a very long time. In fact, forever."

"I'm not talking to you. I'm talking to my conscience."

I'm not your conscience. I'm tinned tuna. In brine.

"What?" I snapped. "Oh, forget it. You're a useless conscience anyway. What good have you done? Nothing, apart from make me feel bad."

I'm trying to tell you, Jasper! I'm an angler fish.

"Whatever."

To my surprise, I felt Mr Pinstripe pat my side. "There, there. No need to get distressed. We all have to follow commands, you know."

I shook my eyestalks at him. "That's the thing, Mr Pinstripe. We don't. Or rather, you don't. Look, why don't you just let me go? I've not done anything *that* bad."

Mr Pinstripe pondered the matter. "Actually, you vandalised a security camera, trespassed into a high security area, impersonated a doctor and then stole the identity of the Emperor of Andromeda."

"But still. You could let me go. Drop me on the nearest planet. Just tell the Emperor I escaped."

"I'm afraid the nearest planet is Inferno V," Pinstripe said, gesturing out of the window at a fiery ball flying past on our right. "Oh, and here we are at Captivon. Sorry—out of time."

The lift slowed as it entered a throbbing silver force field.

"You are now entering the prison planet of Captivon," announced a deep and powerful voice. "Take a look at the stars, for it will be your last."

"So dramatic," Pinstripe murmured appreciatively. "Really creates that atmosphere of eternal incarceration, doesn't it?"

The lift moved slowly through the force field and into a metallic tunnel portioned off into sections by a series of thick metal gates. At each gate there was a pause while the lift was scanned, after which the gates opened and we proceeded to the next one. The level of security was already alarming, but I wasn't going to let Pinstripe know I was scared.

"Bit over the top, isn't it?" I remarked. "Nobody will want to come and visit me at this rate."

Pinstripe patted me again. "Good to see you keeping so cheerful. It will stand you in good stead when you're mouldering in a cell staring at nothing for the rest of your life. A positive outlook is the key to a happy existence, I always feel."

My cheery smile dropped, and I tried not to count as we passed through the eleventh gate.

Finally, we reached a door labelled 'Processing'. It slid open and Pinstripe shook my tail politely with a lower limb.

"Well, good luck. It was nice meeting you. All the best, mind how you go."

"Mr Pinstripe, you seem so nice. Have you ever thought about crossing over to the good side?"

Pinstripe appeared to be thinking for a moment. "Hmm… I have to say no, not really. I love the style of evil—the suits, the tailoring. Look at this fabric." He pointed to a deep maroon velvet waistcoat beneath his suit. "Good always seemed a bit dull in that respect. But who knows?" He smiled at me. "Good luck, anyway."

I slid out slowly, aided by the butt of a laser gun. As the lift zoomed back through the many gates, I saw the guards wave and pretend to cry in an exaggerated way. Despite being so annoying, I didn't want them to go. It meant I was on my own. On my own in an Andromedan prison, where no one could ever find me.

The door slid shut. I waited in the cold, dark, empty metal room to be processed—whatever that meant. I had a hunch it wouldn't be pleasant.

"Name?" a scary voice boomed out.

"Barfbrain," I said rebelliously. They weren't getting anything out of me.

"Crimes?"

"Being better-looking than the Emperor."

"Length of sentence?"

"Five minutes."

"Nice try, Slime Prince. Prepare to be cleansed by the Sanomatic Deep-cleanse Autowasher, the shower that rinses you right through, from the inside out."

There was a rippling feeling in the air, and a wavering, metallic noise that set my teeth on edge. It got louder and louder, feeling like it was going right through me. I put my hands to my ears, and then the sounds died away leaving an emptiness hanging in the air. I took my hands away from my ears and looked at them.

I had hands.

I had ears.

"I'm human-shaped again," I gasped.

"That's the Sanomatic Deep-cleanse Autowasher for you. No hiding behind fake identities here. We've seen them all. Except what's just happened to you… Interesting."

A loud clang came from above as a hatch opened and a set of pyjama-like clothes with arrows on them dropped onto me. It took me ages to get dressed as I had forgotten how to use my arms and legs.

"It's not that difficult," said the voice with a sigh.

"You try putting on prison garb when you've

recently been living as a slug," I snapped.

"Maybe I just will."

I was getting really annoyed with that voice.

With a whine, the back wall slid open and I tottered into a metal waiting room, feeling very high up as I balanced on my long, stick-like legs. Already I was appreciating that life had been so much easier as a slug. Well it certainly wasn't going to be easy now. I felt my eyes sting a little, and then there was a tickle against my neck.

"Fluffy? How in the name of slime did you survive all that?" I gave the little chap a tickle. "You must be indestructible or something." Fluffy nuzzled into me, looking slightly traumatised but very well groomed, like it had had a wash and blow dry. "I'm glad you're here, anyway."

I walked around the room. Iron benches were placed around iron coffee tables with iron bunches of flowers on them. 'Captivon—voted Andromeda's most secure prison planet for the 1000th year running!' announced an engraved sign on the wall.

Next to it, another engraving boasted about Captivon's famous prisoners: the Mind Controlling Mist of Boalf, Orien the 'Orrible, Cheeky Charlie the Intergalactic Pickpocket, and the Slime Prince of Gloop.

Wait a minute. The Slime Prince of Gloop? But that was me. How had they known I was coming? This engraving looked years old; parts of it had rubbed away. And then I realised: I had been here before, when I was a baby. This was obviously the very prison Bill had rescued me from before he'd brought me to Earth and become my foster father.

I was back where it had all begun.

10

TURNS OUT MY CONSCIENCE ISN'T SPEAKING TO ME AFTER ALL

What an idiot I was. It was as though the last eleven years had never happened. Bill had gone to all that trouble to rescue me from here when I was a baby and I had gone and put myself right back again. And this time, there was no Bill. Just me and the worst prisoners in Andromeda. I stared around me with trepidation as a three-headed robot prison guard led me down a metal corridor lined with cells. Fluffy had squirmed under my clothes and sat on my shoulder, hidden but trembling. The weird thing was that none of the cells had doors, only a thin red light around the entrance which hummed quietly.

"Morning, young man!" said a polite prisoner as

we passed. She looked wizened and gaunt, but she still had a cheery smile.

"Welcome—good to meet you," said a man in neatly ironed prison clothes and combed-down hair, giving me a nod.

Not exactly what I'd expected.

The robo-guard stopped abruptly at an empty cell. It aimed a little zapper at it, and the red light appeared around this one too. A loud buzz sounded as I walked reluctantly through it.

"DNA lock successful," the robo-guard said, returning the zapper to a slot on its side.

"What's a DNA lock?"

"Try to escape and you'll find out," Triple Tin Heads said, its other two heads emitting a mechanical laugh.

I stretched out a finger towards the doorway and felt a jolt. "Aaaargh! What was that?"

"Electric shock. Good, eh? Try putting your whole body through, you'll end up as tonight's grilled special. Enjoy your stay."

I wanted to think of something witty and devastatingly cool to say, but my mind was suddenly blank. All I could look forward to was a lifetime of misery. I comforted myself with the fact that the guard was just a robot anyway. My sparkling repartee would be wasted on a mechanical mind. It probably couldn't even hold a conversation.

"Any last words?" intoned the robo-guard, looking at me expectantly with its middle head while the others surveyed each end of the corridor.

"No," I sighed.

"Go on, impress me. Throw me an insult. Anything."

"I can't think of one."

"Shame. I like a bit of banter. Breaks up the day a bit. You might not think it, but it gets quite boring here."

"Hang on—you're a robot. Robots don't get bored."

"Well thank you," the robo-guard said sarcastically. "Robots don't get bored. Robots don't

have emotions. We're just soulless automatons, is that right?"

"Well, yes."

"Cheers. Thanks a bunch. You really know how to make a guy feel good."

"Don't try to make me feel guilty. You're the one who just locked me up in here. Oh, and I've thought of something to say. Rust in peace!"

It was too late. The robo-guard had stomped off in a huff.

I was too late for everything. Too late to stop the Emperor, too late to help Holly, too late to save myself. As for the adoption party, it had probably been cancelled days ago. Maybe Mary and Bill were looking for me and Holly right now. But even if they were, they would never find me here.

I slumped down into the corner of my cell, onto a white outline of a bed. That's right, it was just a drawing. The cell was bare apart from the outlines of a bed, a sink and a bucket. It was worse than having nothing, somehow. My body felt segmented and weak, the floor cold and metallic. Fluffy huddled closer to me.

Jasper. Jasper!

"I told you to go away, conscience. You've been useless so far. If I had to rate you out of ten, it would be a one for turning up and that's it."

It's not your conscience. I told you. It's me, halibut.

"Yep, still useless."

No! It's really hard speaking to you from the eighth dimension. My words keep coming out fish.

The eighth dimension? "Bill, is that you?"

Look up.

I raised my eyes to the metal ceiling which was suddenly filled with swirling colours. Somewhere in there was Bill's face. I could see an eye moving around.

"Bill! But you're all mixed up."

Really? It makes total sense here.

A surge of hope brought a lump to my throat. "Bill, you've been to this prison before. Can you get me out again? Tell me how you knocked out the guard again."

Manta ray whale shark clown fish DNA lock new feature since my time. Sorry.

It didn't sound good. I slumped back down onto my bed—for bed, read floor. "Are there a lot of fish in the eighth dimension or what?"

Actually fish are from *the eighth dimension. The bit you can see is just the tiny part of them that shows up in our own three-dimensional universe.*

"I understood all of that! Well, the words anyway."

Turbot!

Bill began to float around, generating some weird and wonderful colours. For a moment, I thought I saw a shade that didn't actually exist.

"Bill? What's happening?"

Sorry. Got distracted for a moment. Don't know how long I can stay. It's the kippers.

It was really frustrating trying to communicate with Bill, but I was still glad he was here. In his own way, he was a prisoner as well. With a wink of his single eye, Bill swirled down the walls and made patterns under my feet. Considerately, he formed himself into a rectangle under the bed picture, like a colourful duvet.

"Thanks for being here, Bill."

Krill.

I yawned and closed my eyes. It had been a long day. "Does that mean, 'You're welcome'?" I asked sleepily, curling up on him.

No, it's what they call me here. Krill.

Bill—or Krill—went quiet. I tried to sleep, but even Bill's colours couldn't convince my back that it wasn't really lying on a sheet of metal. I got up and went to the door. This time I tried putting a foot through. An electric shock pulsed through me. Stupid to think anything had changed. I fell on the floor in agony and wiggled about for a moment.

"Animal, vegetable or mineral?" said an ancient voice that seemed to come from the wall to my right.

"What?"

"Animal, vegetable or mineral? I'm trying to

guess who you are. I'm in the cell next door. Can't see you, you see."

"I'm Jasper—"

"Don't tell me! Just answer yes or no. Animal, vegetable or mineral."

"Yes."

"You're allowed to answer that one. But only yes or no to the others."

"Animal."

The old man sighed dramatically.

"Sorry, have I disappointed you or something?"

"No, no. I'm sorry. It's just, I wish for once that somebody would answer mineral. But they never do."

"But that would be, like, a rock or something."

"Exactly! Something different. Everybody in here is some sort of humanoid. Same old, same old."

"If you'd asked me earlier, you might have been surprised."

"What?"

"Never mind. Well? Aren't you going to ask me the next question?"

"Another question? In one day? My dear chap, if I do that what on earth will I do tomorrow?"

I supposed I could see his point, although it seemed like a very poor form of entertainment to me.

"Do you want to guess who I am?" he asked brightly.

"Prisoner 926?"

"How on earth...?"

"I'm Prisoner 927 and I'm next door."

"Oh. Yes. Of course, I do have a real name, but there's no point you guessing that as I can't remember what it is. By the way, is there someone else in there with you?"

"Nah, just my foster dad, but he's not really here. He's in the eighth dimension."

There was a murmuring from the cells around me, like I'd just confirmed something everyone had been waiting for.

"That didn't take long," someone said over to my left. "Still, gets to us all in the end."

"What does?" I asked.

"She means we all go a bit doolally in the end," the old man explained. "Happens to the best of us. Usually not within the first five minutes of entering our cell, but still. Never mind, everyone's welcome, mad or sane."

"Hear, hear!"

There was another murmur from the cells around us, and the woman opposite me grinned and raised a thumb in greeting. I couldn't understand it. All the prisoners here were so nice. And then I realised. Of course they were nice. They were the enemies of the Emperor, the people he hated most of all. The people who were the complete opposite of him.

"What are you in here for?" I asked the old man, moving nearer to the wall to listen to him.

I heard him clap his hands excitedly. "Guess!"

"No thanks."

"Oh, please. One question a day?"

"Can't you just tell me?"

The old man let out a disappointed sigh. "Alright. I tried to set up a good neighbour scheme in my part of AndroCity. The Emperor heard about it and banned it. I thought I'd got away with it but then I was caught lending my neighbour a cup of sugar. That was forty years ago."

"Forty years?" I exclaimed. "How have you survived?"

"It's not so bad. We help keep each other's spirits up in here. I Spy is a good game."

I hated I Spy. I still do now, even more. "For forty years?"

"It could be worse."

I didn't see how. "Listen, if we find a way to escape, you should all come. A mass breakout! That'll teach the Emperor."

There was a pause. "Wouldn't that be wrong?"

"No! Not when you've been imprisoned for lending someone a cup of sugar."

"That's nothing. Prisoner 912 was convicted of saying 'good morning'. The Emperor believes everyone should have a *bad* morning, not a good morning."

"What about me?" someone further down called. "I was put away for helping an old lady cross the road."

"I was imprisoned for holding the door open for someone," shouted out a prisoner on the other side.

The prisoners continued to volunteer their stories, until Prisoner 926 asked me what I'd done to deserve being here. "You seem such a nice young inmate. Did you help a stranger by giving them directions? Or make a family member a cup of tea without them asking?"

I considered my list of crimes. Vandalism, trespassing, impersonating the Emperor. Perhaps it was too soon to share. "Er, something like that." Time to change the subject. "Have any of you ever tried to escape?"

Prisoner 926 barked out a brief laugh. "Not likely. DNA locks on every door. Once you've entered, you can never leave."

"What about disguises? Leaving dressed as a washerwoman. That always works in the books."

"Washerwoman? My dear fellow, do you really think we get our washing done for us?"

I sniffed the air, then wished I hadn't. "No, I guess not."

"Besides, it's all done by matching the door to your DNA. Once you're in your cell, you're in it forever, or until the Emperor decides it's zappy-zappy time."

My mind began to race. "So the only way to leave..."

"Would be to change your DNA. You'd have to be able to change into an aardvark or something to get out of here. Even with the beard it still recognises me."

"Thank you. I think you've just saved my life."

I walked into the middle of the cell. It didn't take long—just one step.

Now I had a few more steps to remember—the seven steps to becoming a slug. It had been a while since I'd done it. I'd spent most of my time recently trying *not* to be a slug. Now I was intending to become a slug again. But what if I couldn't return to human form afterwards? I banished that thought from my mind. At least I would be free. Better to be a free slug than an imprisoned boy.

"Right," I told myself bracingly. "Step number one." What was it again? Did it start with the tail, or with the antennae? I tried both. No, it definitely started with something else. I just couldn't remember what.

Brimming over with frustration, I head-butted my pillow, remembered it was just a white painted outline and doubled over with pain. "Ow!"

That was goldfish.

"Thanks, Bill. I mean, Krill. You're a big help."

Bill drifted back up onto the ceiling.

Salmon.

"That's okay, I know you're only trying to help."

Bill's single eye crinkled with an encouraging smile.

"What's it like, in the eighth dimension?" I asked.

Bill replied with a list of fish, but he looked happy.

"I really hope you come back," I told him. "We were going to be a family: you, Mary, me and Hols. Now we're scattered over time and space."

Bill swirled comfortingly around. I watched his colours merge and separate. Suddenly I wondered if I would ever see him in this dimension again.

"Bill, I have to tell you something while I still can. It was me who left the guest room door open. I was the one who should have been chased around the garden by a rabid Mother Fluffian, not you. I'm sorry."

Bill stopped swirling.

Flounder.

"And you know when you couldn't find your electric toothbrush? I was using it as a light sabre."

Thinking of things to apologise for was reminding me of all the good times we had had. Putting Holly's socks in the dishwasher. Using Mary's yoga ball to play Raiders of the Lost Space Ark. Were those times really gone forever?

I rose up with a surge of determination. I was not

going to let the Emperor stop me from having a family. I was going to escape, no matter what it took. I went too close to the door frame and gave myself another electric shock.

"Aaargh!" My human body was getting a really bad welcome back party.

"Are you alright, young sir?" asked Prisoner 926. "Wait, don't tell me. Let me guess."

"I'm fine," I gasped, straightening up.

"Bother. That could have passed the time for months."

"Sorry. But you don't need to pass the time. I'm going to help us all escape."

"By changing into an aardvark?" Prisoner 926 wheezed at his own joke.

"Sort of, yes."

"He really has gone dolally," said another voice.

"I'm afraid so," the old man said, becoming serious again. "Animal, vegetable or mineral, you'll be here until you die. But don't worry, we've got something to help you pass the time. Your turn,

Prisoner 910!"

From far down the corridor, I heard a sing-song voice. "I spy, with my little eye, something beginning with F."

"Floor?" someone else shouted.

"Yes! Well done. Your go, Prisoner 914."

"I spy, with my little eye, something beginning with W."

"Wall?"

"Yes! Congratulations. Your go, Prisoner 935."

"I spy, with my little eye…"

"Shut up!" I yelled. Luckily it was inside my head. I didn't want to ruin the polite atmosphere.

I listened as the prisoners guessed C for ceiling and P for prison before starting on F for floor again. I supposed it wasn't their fault. They just didn't have enough raw material to work with. Maybe I would grow to love I Spy too. I would have to. Otherwise it would be unbearable.

I felt the urge to flick my tail with anger and frustration. But I didn't have a tail anymore.

"Bill," I moaned. "Help me turn into a slug!"

I looked up for the comforting swirl of Bill's presence.

But he had disappeared.

11

TURNS OUT FLUFFY'S GOT A HIDDEN SIDE...

It seemed impossible that I would fall asleep on the picture of a bed, but I did. There was no tea, telly, quarrel with Holly and then bed, which was my usual routine. I didn't even have to clean my teeth. It didn't feel right. I longed to do something normal, like ask Bill for a cup of water a million times. I couldn't even ask Eighth Dimension Bill. He had dissolved back into his own strange reality, leaving me solidly stuck in mine.

Not that any of this was his fault. No, it was all my own doing. I had rushed off without giving a thought to how it might all turn out. And it was my fault that Holly had come after me. And after all her hard work, the Emperor had pressed the button anyway. I just had to hope that she had been able to brainwash the clones even a little bit. Otherwise the Earth was doomed and I had done absolutely nothing to stop it happening. From now on, I decided, I would be like a wise mystic, or a sage, floating around ruminating on every possibility before acting. I would wear long flowing white robes and hum to myself. I would be patient and kind, and think of other people before myself. I would change.

I woke up to a familiar sound.

"I spy with my little eye…"

"Shut up!" Oops. This time I had said it out loud. "Please," I begged. "I can't stand it."

"Sorry," Prisoner 926 said cheerfully through the walls. "We're just killing the time until breakfast."

"Breakfast? We get breakfast?" This was great news. Even with the prospect of facing the rest of my life in prison playing I Spy, I was starving.

"Well, we call it breakfast."

That didn't sound very promising.

I heard the *clank, clank* of metal feet approaching and a chorus of polite thank yous as Triple Tin Heads worked its way down the corridor before appearing at my door with a tray. Its two peripheral heads were keeping watch on the outside corridor, as usual.

"Great, room service!" I said cheerfully. "I'd like beans on toast, please. Timz, not Jimz. Boiled so they're nice and soft and mushy. And dark toast, almost burned but not quite."

"Very funny." The robo-guard clonked into my cell and put the tray on the ground. On it was a metal cup of water and a metal plate with a flat grey rectangle in the middle.

"What's this?"

"Human-Dins."

"It's grey."

"Human-Dins contains all necessary ingredients to prolong life, with no added taste or flavour."

"You're really selling it to me."

The robo-guard put a hand on its hip. "Listen, it's not my fault. I'm just the messenger."

"You mean there's a chef?"

"There's a machine. Human-Dins comes out of one end. And into the other end—"

"No, don't tell me. I don't want to know what goes into it."

"Correct decision."

I stared at the grey rectangle that looked like a lump of squashed clay. "Thanks. Oh, and rust in peace."

"You said that yesterday."

The robo-guard clonked off to the next cell where I heard Prisoner 926 receive his tray with a burst of enthusiastic gratitude.

"What does it taste like?" I called through the wall.

"Guess."

I took a bite. There was no flavour at all, but the texture was disgusting. "Jimz Beans."

"I was going to give you a clue!" Prisoner 926 moaned.

I finished my meal with difficulty and went to freshen up at the 'sink' before remembering that it wasn't real. I could see why the prisoners had retreated into a semi-imaginary world. It was the only way to survive. But it wasn't for me. I had to get out before another game of I Spy started. I needed to think of a way to escape using only the few resources I had at my disposal: some two-dimensional pictures of furniture, the ability to turn into a slug which I didn't have at the moment and half a Human-Dins that even Fluffy was turning its nose up at. It was so frustrating. I really missed my tail. I just wanted to thump it on the ground and let everyone know how angry I was...

Thump!

I looked down. It was happening. My body was growing thicker. I felt the segmented parts of me form together into one mass.

"I'm a slug!" I yelled.

There was a groan around me and a lot of muttering about how I could have just let them guess

what had happened.

Quickly I slid towards the doorway and the glowing red frame. I stuck an eyestalk through, waiting for the sickening sizzle. Nothing. It had worked! Gingerly I moved the rest of my body through the gap and out into the corridor. I got some strange looks from the other prisoners but they were too polite to comment. And I didn't care—I was free!

Well, free to go in and out of my cell at will anyway. I didn't have a clue how I would get off the prison planet. Or how I would rescue the others, because I wasn't leaving without them. They were too nice to leave here to rot, even if they were extremely annoying at times. I had to deactivate their DNA locks somehow. Then I remembered: Triple Tin Heads had that zappy thing which had turned my door lock on. Perhaps it worked with all the others as well. I just needed to get it off him.

I zoomed back into my cell where my Human-Dins tray lay on the ground, thrown there in disgust.

I tucked my tail around it and tried to pick it up. It wasn't easy. But what else did I have to knock out the robo-guard? That's what Bill had done in his day. But Bill had had *hands*, my common sense reminded me.

I practised a bit more—after all, I would have to do it three times, one for each head— then lay on my bed, a bit more comfy now that I had a thick layer of slug blubber around me, and waited for the arrival of Triple Tin Heads. Luckily it wasn't long before I heard the now familiar *clank, clank* of approaching metal feet. This time it was accompanied by lighter footsteps, although still quite heavy, as though the person was stamping.

"Sounds like a new prisoner!" Prisoner 926 announced in an excited voice. "Don't tell me what lifeform they are! I'm going to make this one last as long as possible."

Voices were raised. It sounded like the new prisoner was arguing with the robo-guard. That had to be unusual for this place. I listened carefully, in

case the prisoner caused a problem in my carefully laid—or actually just hastily bashed together—plan. After all, if the plan succeeded then they would be free as well. The idea of being set free in the company of a psychopathic killer wasn't very appealing.

"And I'm telling you that if I don't get that t-shirt back when I leave I'll be complaining in writing. That was Harry Handsome's face on there, in case you didn't know. Oh, what am I talking about? Robots can't appreciate music. They don't have those sorts of emotions."

The clanging noise stopped; the robo-guard must have halted. My heart was leaping. It was Holly! I couldn't have been more happy to hear that she was about to be locked in a maximum security prison— for the sake of the plan, of course, not because she had once stepped on my Cosmos Wars BlackStar Battleship and never apologised.

"Say that again?" Triple Tin Heads was saying, a belligerent tone in its voice.

"I'm sorry, but you don't have emotions. Hang on, why am I even apologising? You don't have emotions to be offended."

"I actually feel quite offended by that comment now, as well as the other one."

"Don't believe you. You could be programmed to say that."

"How dare you! This is genuine emotion I'm feeling."

Great. Old Metal Brains was distracted. I flicked the tray up onto my tail and stuck an eyestalk out to check out the situation. The robo-guard had his back to me. I slid out, slowly. Holly was facing towards me, wearing prison clothing which she was obviously hating. She had her hands on her hips and looked furious. When she saw me over the robo-guard's shoulder she did a double-take, but one only I would have noticed. I slid silently nearer.

"Prove it," Holly said. "Cry."

"But I'll rust!"

"I don't care. I'll believe you if, and only if, you

shed real tears."

Triple Tin Heads sighed. "Oh, alright then. Just give me a minute."

I was very close now. I could actually see the zapper, sitting in a little metal pocket on the robo-guard's right hand side. I lifted the tray with my tail.

CLANG!

It fell to the floor.

The robo-guard spun round. All three heads had their eyes closed and its hands were over its middle set. "Stop trying to put me off!" it wailed.

I went to push the tray towards Holly, nodding at the robo-guard's heads, but she shook her own in an I-have-a-plan way.

"Bet it gets lonely working here," she said in a sympathetic voice. "All alone on this massive planet. Only a load of prisoners who hate you."

"We don't hate you!" called out the woman in the opposite cell.

"Don't listen to them!" Holly said quickly. "They don't understand you. Nobody does. About how sad you feel when you think about… a little boy who's lost his favourite teddy. A tiny puppy who wants his mum."

The robo-guard began to make strange gulping noises.

"A poor little kitten lost in the snow."

The robo-guard broke into open sobs. "A newly manufactured bot who's lost his motherboard!" it blubbered.

I saw Holly's face light up as she elaborated on how much the bot missed his motherboard. The robo-guard hunched over, wailing. I stopped bothering trying to hide behind it—it was too distraught to notice me. Huge tears poured out of all three of its heads. They trickled down its necks and into an air vent on its chest. There was a sizzling sound followed by a loud pop. All three heads dropped and became still.

"Nope, I'm still not convinced," Holly said. "It could just be clever programming." She grinned at me.

"That was brilliant," I said. "Much better than knocking him out with a tray three times."

"That was your plan?"

Before we knew what we were doing we had hugged and then, because we never did hug, we stepped back from each other and looked embarrassed.

"Emperor Blobby pressed the ring," I told her. "The portals have opened."

Holly nodded. "I know. I just hope I did enough. Some of the Harrys had become so nice they wouldn't even get in the portals. But some did."

"So it might have worked?"

"I guess we'll find out. I tried to get into a portal as well but they arrested me just as I put a leg through. I'm lucky to be in one piece. Is this your cell?"

I showed Holly around, then made my preparations to leave.

"What are you doing?" Holly demanded.

"Making my bed. I want to leave things nice."

Holly grabbed my arm. "You've been here too

long. You're institutionalised."

"But—"

"It's a picture. And stop cleaning the sink! Let's get out of here." Holly groaned. "What are you looking for now?"

"Nothing," I said quickly, but it was too late. Sensing we were leaving, Fluffy was zooming about in full view looking slightly panicked.

Holly shook her head. "Oh, Jasper. That's kidnapping!"

"I tried to get rid of Fluffy, I really did. It just follows me everywhere." Fluffy hopped onto my tail and settled down, looking relieved. "To be honest, I don't think I could have survived without it."

Holly bent down and gave the little blue creature a tickle. I heard a tiny chuckling sound. "Thanks, Fluffy," Holly said.

It was very quiet in the corridor. Just us and the robo-guard, slumped forward with smoke coming out of its chest. The prisoners were staring at us in horror.

"That wasn't very nice," Prisoner 926 said in a reproving tone.

"It's not like it's dead," I explained. "It probably just needs oiling."

"No, I mean about the kitten. I'm very upset."

Holly and I went around consoling the prisoners as we set them free. It was fun pressing the zapper and seeing their amazed faces as they stepped out of their cells for the first time in years. Most of them had a lot of facial hair and were quite elderly. I hoped we could get them to safety and some sort of life.

We checked the robo-guard's body again and found some keys, helpfully labelled 'Robot Relaxation Room', 'Broom Cupboard' and 'Don't Let the Prisoners Get Hold of This One'. Feeling more optimistic about our chances of escape, we marched back to the reception area.

"Do us a favour," I asked Holly, spotting a pot of 'I've Escaped from Captivon!' souvenir biros. I watched as she crossed my name off the list of famous prisoners and scrawled, 'ESCAPED!' next to it in giant letters.

"Happy now? Then let's get out of here." Holly studied the robo-guard's 'Don't Let the Prisoners Get Hold of This One' key. "I guess this is the one," she said, pressing the green button. A sliding door began to open with a whine.

"I spy with my little eye, something beginning with F," Prisoner 926 said in a tremulous voice.

"Floor?" someone suggested enthusiastically.

"No. Freedom!"

There was a cheer and a few sobs. I felt a tear pulse behind my eye, but maybe it was just the thought of another game of I Spy starting up.

Suddenly, from behind us, there was a massive *clang*.

"Guess what emotion I'm feeling now!" the three-headed guard roared. There was still smoke coming out of its chest but otherwise it looked fine.

"Bother," Holly said. It was actually something much ruder but I won't write it here.

"Ooh! I know! Pick me, pick me!" The prisoners all raised their hands. Some of them started jumping up and down.

Triple Tin Heads looked round for a moment, then pointed at me. And I didn't even have my hand up. The other prisoners sighed with disappointment and I got several dark looks.

"Anger?" I suggested.

"I don't believe you're feeling anything at all," Holly said dismissively. "You're just following the instructions of your creators. You can't act independently even if you tried."

"Can't I?" The robo-guard pulled out two massive laser guns.

"Oops."

I groaned. "Thanks for goading it into killing us, Hols."

Triple Tin Heads raised its guns. "The Emperor wanted you alive so he could zap you at his leisure, but I'm going to save him the bother and do it now. Prepare to meet your circuit makers!"

I felt a tickle behind my neck, and a tiny blue fluffy ball bounced over my shoulder and onto the ground. It rolled towards Triple Tin Heads and let out a tiny roar, no louder than a kitten.

"Fluffy, no!"

"Think I'm frightened of that? Haven't you got anything better? Ha ha ha!" the robo-guard crowed, taking turns to laugh with each of its heads.

"Thanks anyway, Fluffy," I told it. "It's the thought that counts—whoa!"

Fluffy had puffed up to the size of a baby elephant. Its blue fur was sticking out at crazy angles and it was displaying two rows of very sharply pointed teeth.

"Rooooaaaaaaaaaaaarrrrrrrr!" it roared.

Triple Tin Heads ran shrieking down the metal corridor and back towards the bowels of the prison, the *clank, clank* of its feet faster than I had ever heard them.

"I'm convinced," Holly said. "I think it really does feel emotion. You can't fake that scream."

Through the newly opened door was the processing room. Holly pressed another button on the key. The door whined open and we moved into the long metal corridor and its endless gates, stretching on for what seemed like forever. We still had a long way to go.

"Guess what I need?" Prisoner 926 groaned, leaning against the wall.

"A rest?" I suggested. "That's good, because I need to pop back a moment. Wait here for me, Hols. Fluffy—try to deflate. I'm not carrying you around like that."

Fluffy looked confused and zoomed off into a wall. It had obviously surprised itself as well as everyone else.

"But where are you—" Holly began, but I was already sliding back to the processing room.

"Anybody there?" I asked.

"Oh, it's you," said the voice. "Barfbrain, wasn't it?"

"Yes. Sorry I didn't say hi on the way through.

We were in a bit of a hurry."

"People usually are around here," the voice said philosophically. "But then they stick around for a long time. It doesn't make sense. But it's not my job to wonder. I just do the cleansing."

"Yes. About that. I was just wondering if you could do that to me again."

"Again?"

"Yes. Just like you did the first time."

"That's very unusual."

"But not a problem?"

"I suppose not. Very well. Prepare to be cleansed by the Sanomatic Deep-cleanse Autowasher, the shower that rinses you right through, from the inside out."

"Are you being paid for product placement or something?"

I felt the familiar tugs and bulges as my poor old body changed shape yet again. I stretched out my human arms and legs one by one, and found my old clothes on a hook. "Thanks."

"For what it's worth, I think you looked better before."

"Charming."

I hobbled back to the others, getting used to my new limbs again.

"Interesting," Holly said, folding her arms and waiting for an explanation.

"The prison helped," I explained. "Turns out it's not too bad around here when you know how things work."

Once the escaped prisoners had rested and Fluffy had reverted to its normal size or slightly bigger (it was puffed up a bit with pride), we began trudging down the metal corridor. The euphoria of escaping wore off as we passed gate after gate, moving through the security system of the Emperor's prison. There was nothing to relieve the monotony, apart from...

"I hear, with my little ear, something beginning with S."

I was beginning to learn that you could always

rely on Prisoner 926 to double the boredom factor.

"Sounds?" I suggested listlessly.

"No, a spaceship!"

We all stopped and listened.

"We have to flag it down, but we'll never make it to the last gate in time," I groaned. "Holly, how many more?"

"How should I know? I just press the button." Holly aimed the key at the next gate. It opened to reveal the star-studded blackness of space. "Oh, right. One."

"Hurray!" We all cheered and rushed towards the gap, then realised we weren't rushing—we were being sucked out into the vacuum of space.

"Heeeeeeeeelp!" I tried to scream, but couldn't. What an ending, after getting this far. I wasn't sad to be dying—I didn't have time for that—just extremely annoyed. I could see the others drifting away from the exit and towards the stars. We were all going in different directions. "Hollyyyyy! Fluffyyyyy! Come baaaaack!"

Suddenly I heard a loud announcement. It came from a tiny ship which was now floating not far from Captivon's entrance.

"This is Flarp Moonchaser, Slayer of the Multi-Headed Muck Monster of Murg, retired customer service executive at the Galactic Tourist Office and all round space-hero. I have been reliably informed by a visitor from the eighth dimension that you are holding the Slime King of Gloop. Release the prisoner or prepare to go to war. I can destroy this place with the press of a button." There was a pause. "Wait a minute. I can see them drifting by my windscreen. Marvellous. Not to worry. I'll sort this one out myself."

It was Flarp! The ship was tiny, but it had to be hers. I wondered how much breath I had left in me. It didn't feel like much. I didn't think it would be enough to get to the ship, anyway, even if I could direct myself. But maybe some of the others would make it. Maybe Holly would. I hoped she would remembered to say some nice things about me after my death. Knowing her, it was unlikely. Fluffy might, if only it could speak...

SCHLUP!

What looked like a massive vacuum cleaner nozzle appeared from the side of the ship. I felt a sudden immense pull and a rushing feeling. The next moment, I was thrown into a chamber of the ship, the opening had closed off and air (wonderful air) was pouring in. I gulped it down and did a quick head count. Everyone was here. Holly and I did a wordless thumbs up and Fluffy whizzed to my neck and nuzzled in gratefully.

"Everybody here?" said Flarp's voice through a speaker. "Quite a lot of you, aren't there? Is this a prison break? Never mind, any enemy of the Emperor is a friend of mine."

A few minutes later, when we had all recovered, we went through an air hatch and into Flarp's spaceship. I'd expected a big battle cruiser-type thing with stacks of room and loads of weapons. Turns out Flarp's ship was a small round bubble with one room. We stood shoulder to shoulder while Flarp busied herself at the controls.

"Sorry about the squash, old chums. My breakdown insurance entitles me to a free replacement spaceship, but only the cheapest sort."

"But you said you could destroy Captivon with just the press of a button," I pointed out.

"They weren't to know it wasn't true, were they? Anyway, in the end you did the hard bit. I'm just here to take you to Earth. There's been a bit of bother down there."

Holly and I looked at each other nervously.

"Is it anything to do with the checkouts at Asbi's?" I asked.

"And an army of clones?" Holly said.

"I knew it wouldn't work," I added bitterly. "All that for nothing."

Flarp pushed a lever and we hurtled away from Captivon at an alarming speed. "I don't know about any of that," she said, hanging some fluffy dice above the windscreen, "but it seems the whole of

Little Blanding knows the lyrics to 'It's a Wonderful World (With Me In It)'."

"Does that mean it's worked?" I asked Holly.

"I hope so. Even I'm sick of that song now," Holly admitted, gripping a pull-out handle as we watched Captivon disappear for good. "I guess we'll find out very soon."

12

TURNS OUT FISH ARE OUR OVERLORDS

Earth was a bit different when we got back. Well, Little Blanding was at least, and reports on the news backed up Flarp's information that the same thing was happening at every other town or village in the country with an Asbi's. The Harrys had arrived through the self-service tills and were spreading their vision: a dream of a world full of peace, love and harmony. Asbi's claimed it was a publicity stunt, sponsored by Harry Handsome himself. I had to admire their quick thinking. Perhaps a Harry had suggested the idea to them, or maybe it was the brainwashed fans who had insisted on working there—although they didn't seem to be brainwashed anymore as they were all leaving.

It was exactly the opposite of what the Emperor had intended. The Harry 'tribute acts', as people thought of them, were making the country a better place. Maybe that would put him off invading Earth for a while. Maybe.

"Do you think we did the right thing?" I asked Holly as we walked through the village. The sun was setting behind the clock tower sending pinky rays across the tops of the trees. It was the perfect evening for our adoption party.

Holly shrugged. "What else could we have done? Sometimes brainwashing clones is the only solution. Besides, Mary said we did okay."

I grimaced, remembering. Mary had actually been pretty angry with us, and when I thought about what we'd done—running off into outer space *again*—I couldn't really blame her. But, when she met us on the roof as Flarp finally touched down in Little Blanding, she was too full of relief and happiness to show it. In fact, she never did show it.

She just told us. As she was hugging us.

"I'm so cross with you two!"

"Then why are you laughing?" Holly asked her.

"I'm allowed to be cross and happy at the same time." Mary stopped hugging us for a moment. "Now will you promise me not to keep making a habit of this?"

Holly and I looked at each other. "Er…" we both began.

Mary gave us a warning look. "We'll discuss this later. And who are all these people?"

"Guess!" Prisoner 926 bounded up enthusiastically, his beard waving in the night breeze.

Mary looked him up and down. "Escaped prisoners from Captivon? Your prison outfit has a logo."

Prisoner 926 shook his head. "Blast!"

"We had to help them," Holly explained. "They were imprisoned for the crime of being nice."

Mary did a quick headcount. "It's going to be a squeeze."

"I don't think you'll get any complaints," I told her.

Mary was brilliant. She arranged with Flarp to find homes for all the escaped prisoners on Gloop. When I heard, I offered the Slime Palace. There was plenty of room with me not being there. I also told Mary all about meeting Bill in the ceiling of the prison, and how he had helped me. That made Mary look sad, because she hadn't seen him since their experiments on the roof had gone wrong. And after all that work, the Greater Multessimal family of Sproing had never turned up.

"Maybe Bill just appears when you really need him?" I suggested. "Like a superhero."

"That's a nice thought," Mary said.

"Do you think he'll ever go back to being normal?" I asked. Eighth Dimension Bill was cool, but he couldn't give me a hug or unclog the sink.

Mary laughed. "Bill was never normal. That's why I married him. But yes, I hope so. Flarp and I are doing lots of research. Don't give up just yet."

"I won't," I said fiercely. "Not ever."

But Bill hadn't turned up, and now it was the

evening of the adoption party. Mary had changed her mind about us helping as she said it was going to be a surprise. The surprise to me was that it was happening at all after everything that had gone on, but Mary said she and Bill would never have changed their mind about adopting us. Mary had even accepted Fluffy as our official household pet, although she insisted on trying to contact the Mother Fluffian to get her permission. The Fluffians, however, were uncontactable. They were spies for the Emperor, after all. Except Fluffy, of course. Fluffy was definitely on our side. And on my shoulder. I gave it a pat and it chuckled happily.

"Do you need help crossing the road?" asked a silken voice. A Harry, noticing we were approaching the edge of the pavement, had rushed up to help.

"No, thank you," Holly said brusquely.

"It's a wonderful world, isn't it? Shall we all just live in peace?"

"No. I mean, yes. Whatever."

"If you believe in me, I'll believe in you."

Holly stopped in the middle of the road. "Will you just clear off?"

I gasped. "Holly! You've made Harry Handsome cry!"

The Harry's face had crumpled. Holly just marched off and I had to half-run to keep up with her. "I don't care," she said, tossing her head defiantly. "I'm getting sick of them. When it was just one Harry Handsome, it was special. Everyone wanted him. He was rare—one of a kind. Now he's as ordinary as... baked beans."

"Timz or Jimz?"

"Jimz of course. Cheap, low quality and a complete con."

"But we did it, Holly! It worked. We saved the Earth—again!"

Holly sighed. "I guess. I'm just sad. I've lost him, Jasper. It'll never be the same again."

We walked past a Church of Harry, up Harry Road and towards the community centre, which I noticed had been renamed the Harry Handsome

Happy Centre. It was amazing how quickly the Harrys had managed to influence daily life. At the centre, a Harry shook our hands and told us he would be there for us whenever we needed him. Holly just rolled her eyes.

I followed her up the path and into the foyer. The main room looked dark, as though there was nobody there.

"Do you think we've got the right place?" I asked.

"Duh. It's a surprise, isn't it? They're all going to jump out and shout Happy Adoption or something," Holly said. "Come on, put on your surprised face."

Holly didn't look as excited as I felt. "What's wrong?"

"I still didn't get them a present, did I? Too busy saving the Earth."

"I told you: that can be our present."

"Not very personal though, is it? Oh, we got you a present but we got the same for everybody else in the whole world."

"But still. Freedom. I mean, you can't get a better present than that."

"I mean, I can't give them this," Holly continued, pulling a small glass bottle filled with foul-looking green liquid out of her pocket.

I reeled in horror. "Why have you still got that?"

"I thought it might come in useful."

"The Emperor's mump juice? When, exactly?"

"I don't know, I just have a feeling." Holly pocketed the bottle. She always had been a bit weird.

"I don't expect there'll be much of a fuss anyway," I said, trying to forget about mump juice as quickly as possible. "Mary's been too busy looking for us and trying to rescue Bill. I wish she'd let us help." I pushed open the door, not expecting much but hoping Mary had at least had time to make her signature triple-chocolate cake.

"Surprise!" shouted a load of aliens as the hall lit up with colour and noise. At least, I thought they were aliens. Turns out Mary had made it an alien-themed fancy dress party, so anyone looking vaguely non-human could blend in. She was a bit clever like that. Despite the costumes, I made out loads of escaped prisoners. They looked like they were really enjoying themselves at last. Through the streamers and the bunting, I also spotted a long table full of food and my five best friends Chad, Max, Charlie, Ali and Jake all stuffing their faces. They waved at me with fake antennae and three-fingered gloves and continued scoffing.

Flarp came towards me and slapped me on the back. "Happy adoption day, mini Clarkson."

"Thanks Flarp. And thanks for rescuing us."

"No problem, dear newly adopted boy. But you should thank Bill. He was the one who contacted me. I knew that interdimensional communication implant would come in handy one day." She tapped the side of her head where there was a faint scar.

"Well if I ever see him again, I will."

"But that's the surprise! Don't tell me you haven't noticed?" Flarp gestured to a huge tank on the other side of the hall, the sort you see full of tropical fish in restaurants. It seemed to be full of coloured water, but there was something else in there as well.

"Bill!" I called, running towards it. "Bill, is that you?"

"Don't you mean Krill?" said Bill's voice, slightly muffled.

His face and arms were waving around inside the glass. It was good to see him, but painful. It reminded me of how far away he really was. But at least he didn't look as distorted as he had in the prison.

"Surprise!" Mary said, coming up behind me. "It's an Eighth Dimension Tank. Flarp and I invented it. It's a way for Bill to spend time with us. We'll fix it up in the living room. Maybe get rid of the telly." She gazed at Bill serenely. "It's actually very relaxing watching him."

"Yeah," I muttered. "Great." Didn't she understand that I wanted Bill back—the real, three-dimensional Bill?

Mary put her arm round me. "What's wrong, Jasper?"

"Nothing. It's great," I lied. "Thank you. It's the best adoption present ever."

Mary's lips twitched. She glanced at Flarp. Flarp was making a strange face. Her eyes were crossing.

Mary gave a sudden snort. "It's no good, I can't keep it up. Come out, Bill!"

Bill stepped out from behind the tank. "Ta da!" he announced, flinging out his arms.

"You weren't in there at all?"

"Nope."

"You were pretending?"

"Yep."

"So you're back from the eighth dimension after all?"

"Certainly am, kipper. Sorry, still got a few fishy phrases stuck in my brain. But basically yes, I'm back."

I rushed towards Bill and hugged the real three-dimensional him. "I really thought you were in a tank. But it was all a trick." I stepped back and looked at him and Mary. "You two are weird. And now you're my parents."

"And there's nothing you can do about it," Mary said happily. "Shame Holly missed it though."

"Yes, where is she?" Bill asked. "She did come in with you, didn't she?"

Somewhere on the way I had lost Holly. It didn't feel right without her.

"I'll go and look for her," Mary said. "And we have some more special guests to see you." She slipped away, smiling mysteriously.

"So why are there so many fish in the eighth dimension?" I asked Bill.

"Apparently fish are the natural overlords of creation, but they don't like to talk about it."

"They must have done for you to find that out."

"That was the funny thing. Once they do start, they don't shut up."

Mary reappeared carrying what looked like a little green tray. It was a large lettuce leaf, and lying on it were two slugs who were very precious to me.

"Mum! Dad! You made it!"

Mum and Dad reared up, stretching their antenna towards me.

"Your father made a spaceship out of flubber leaves," Mum said proudly.

"Your mother didn't think it would work, but it did," Dad added, even more proudly. "Nothing can keep us away from our son."

"He drove like a maniac."

"I was excited."

"You're supposed to give way when entering the Milky Way bypass."

"It wasn't my fault that road hog cut me up! He was doing well over 10,000 light years an hour."

"The important thing is that you're here," I said.

"Are you sure you didn't want to stay as a slug?" Mum asked.

"Not this time." One day, I would go home to rule my kingdom, but until then I was happy on Earth, being a normal family with Mary, Bill and

Holly and just occasionally saving the Earth from alien invasion.

"Shame. We find the perspective really refreshing. And you're so handsome and glossy in your slug form!" Mum gushed. "But Mary said your hormones were running riot and making your body do all sorts of weird things—"

Before I could interrupt her to change the subject, a voice announced:

"Presenting a tribute to Mary and Bill by Holly Clarkson and the Harry Handsome Singers!"

In came Holly with three Harrys. The Harrys were all talking together excitedly; from their body language it looked like they were exchanging compliments. Holly broke them up and put them in a line.

"One, two, three, four," she chanted, and they all broke into an a cappella rendition of 'It's a Wonderful World (With Me In It)'. Holly sung the verses but with slightly different words. There was stuff about how great Mary and Bill were for putting up with her for so long, and even a little bit about me that wasn't hugely insulting. The only trouble was that in the chorus the Harrys kept insisting on singing the original lyrics 'It's a wonderful world with me in it' rather than Holly's altered lyrics of 'It's a wonderful world with Mary and Bill in it'. Holly got more and more annoyed throughout the song and tried to tell them off without anyone noticing.

Everybody cheered at the end and Mary wiped her eyes with a NASA handkerchief. "That's the best present ever," she sobbed, as Holly admonished the Harrys who were too busy congratulating each other to notice.

"Hang on, what about *my* present?" I demanded. "The gift of freedom?"

"Oh yes, that's definitely up there with my all-time favourite presents too." Mary gave me a squeeze. "I've got something for you two as well. I thought you might like a triple-chocolate cake. Although this one's an eight-layer, in honour of Bill's return."

13

EPILOGUE

One Saturday morning, Holly and I were hanging out in the living room watching kids' cartoons when the doorbell rang.

"You go."

"No, you go."

Mary was in the garden shed working on her interdimensional portal. Since she and Flarp had succeeded in getting Bill back, she had been trying to extend its uses to other dimensions as well. Bill had gone to the local DIY shop to get parts. Now that they weren't taking in lodgers anymore, they were hoping the portal could make our family's fortune instead. Flarp had great contacts with the inter-dimensional community. She and my slug parents had gone back to Gloop together with the ex-prisoners, who were full of gratitude and excitement about their new home. Mary and Bill said we would all go and visit them soon, but for the moment I just wanted to be at home, being normal. Watching cartoons, eating toast and moaning about school. Just for a bit.

The doorbell rang again. I popped the last piece of toast into my mouth and dragged myself up from the floor. "Coming."

The visitor was wearing his trademark leather jacket, white t-shirt and jeans, accessorized with perfect hair and a dazzling smile. I led him into the living room.

"Hols, it's a Harry."

"Whatever." Holly didn't look away from the television. It was odd to see this new Harry-free Holly, but it seemed permanent. Even her dream of dueting with Harry hadn't affected her feelings; they had all much preferred each other's voices to hers.

It had been the last straw.

The Harry stood in front of us, tossing a strand of artfully arranged hair back from his face. "You two have ruined my life," he said moodily. The other Harrys never sounded like that.

"Wait a minute—you're the real Harry?"

"Of course I am! I can't believe no one else can tell." Harry pulled a scrap of paper out of his pockets. "Look. Song lyrics. The others can't come up with anything original. They're just bland copies. You've flooded the Earth with fake Harrys. You've devalued my brand, that's what you've done."

"The Emperor did that. Blame him if you want to blame anyone," Holly said curtly, without a hint of the gooey expression she usually saved for Harry.

"You know what you did. You made them nice." Harry looked disgusted. "These ones just want to sing and help everyone to live together in harmony."

"And that's a bad thing?" I asked.

Harry slumped into a chair. "Please. I'm begging you. I've realised how much my pop career means to me, and to everyone else on Earth. I want it back! I'll go over to the good side, I promise, if you can just get rid of them all. I've even stopped brainwashing my fans, that's how nice I am!"

"Harry, I'd love to help you. But you're the fifth Harry who's turned up today. Four is my absolute limit."

I jerked my thumb to the sofa behind me where a line of Harrys sat, happily preening themselves in front of small mirrors we had given to keep them occupied. I had a feeling these were the original Harrys who hadn't conformed to Professor Placebo's cloning ideals, the ones Holly had reprogrammed to be good and teach the others. They were always dropping in and insisted on following me around, like cats who sat on the lap of the one person in the room that hated them. Oddly, I was starting to get quite fond of them. Unlike the real Harry, they had no egos. Holly had done a good job.

"You can join them if you like," I told Harry, knowing this would infuriate him. "I think they're planning on forming a supergroup."

"But they can't! *I'm* the real Harry!" Harry blurted.

"That's what they all say," Holly said, taking a bite of toast.

"But I am!" Harry was almost crying. His deep brown eyes sparkled with diamond-like tears. Suddenly they lit up. "I'll prove it once and for all," he said, leaping up. "I've got a sample here."

"Ugh! There's no need for that!" I said quickly, raising my hands in protest.

"No, a sample of my new fragrance. It was in development before all this happened and I've got the only prototype. It's called 'Simply Harry'. Tagline: 'Because he's worth it.'" He pulled a fancy little glass bottle out of his pocket.

"Here, let me see." I took the bottle from him. The label said, 'Harry Handsome sample perfume. Tester only. Do not sell'. "Perhaps he is the real Harry," I said to Holly.

Holly jumped up. "There's only one way to tell," she said, winking at me. "If you'll excuse me for a moment, I'll just take this up to my lab." She snatched the bottle from me and ran upstairs.

Harry was momentarily distracted by a T.V. advert for his new album. I heard a glug of pouring liquid upstairs and then Holly reappeared with the perfume, looking smug. Did the bottle look a bit fuller?

"Perhaps he's right," she said, handing it back to Harry. "It does smell a bit like Andromeda." She winked at me again, and I suddenly remembered another little bottle with liquid in.

I stared at her. She hadn't—had she?

"I can't get rid of all the other Harrys, and I'm not going to," I told him. "If you want your career back there's only one thing you can do."

Harry raised a perfectly manicured eyebrow.

"Be better than them. Stand out from the crowd. We'll help you if you like. But I should warn you, the other Harrys are pretty good. And people love your voice. Think how much more they'll love the sound of Harrys harmonising with each other? If you can't beat them, how about joining them?"

"Never!" Harry spat. He stalked to the door. "You wait. I'll be the best Harry there's ever been. I'll be unique."

"Why don't you spray on some of your scent? None of the other Harrys have got that," Holly suggested.

"Good idea." Harry opened the bottle. Holly stepped back. I did too. Could she really have added some of the Emperor's mump juice? "Mmm," he said, spraying some on. His face changed. For the first time ever, Harry Handsome looked more like Harry Horrible. "Actually, I think it needs some work. A lot of work." Looking sickened, he ran out of the room and we heard the front door slam.

Everything had been worth it to get to this moment.

"He always did like being close to the Emperor," Holly remarked with a smug smile. "Now he'll feel really close."

"Do you think he meant it, about coming over to

the good side?"

"No chance. The Emperor's going to find some way of getting back at us, and Harry's bound to be involved. I don't believe a word he said."

"Wow. You've really changed. I don't suppose you want to hear his new song lyrics then," I said, picking the scrap of paper off the carpet where Harry had dropped it.

"No thanks. And I can't believe you're going ahead with this Harry supergroup idea. They'll never accept you as their manager. They're too interested in themselves. They haven't looked up from those mirrors for ages."

"We'll see." I unfolded the paper and read. "*To do list.* That's a good title. Bill would like that! And at least he's not writing about how wonderful he is. Maybe he has changed? Let's see. *Number one – hair appointment. Number two – manicure. Number three – go to Gloop and kidnap the ex-Slime King and Queen...*" I stopped. "Wait a minute—that's my Triangulum mum and dad! These aren't song lyrics at all, are they?"

"Nope." Holly stretched. "Ah well. We've had a few days of peace. And we've got an army of clones to help us now." She snatched the mirrors away from the Harrys. One by one they looked around as though lost, then started beaming at each other and exchanging delighted compliments.

"And we've got Fluffy," I added, patting my shoulder where Fluffy sat gently vibrating. "You get your backpack. I'll get the Harrys' shoes and coats."

"And this time we're telling Mary and Bill. They're our parents now. Okay?"

"Okay."

Fluffy chirruped excitedly. It wasn't over—maybe it would never be over—but we were up for the challenge. We always would be.

The End

Too Handsome by HH

I've never done wrong in my life
I've never caused anyone ~~grief~~ strife
But ask me if I'm pretty
And I'd have to say I'm guilty

CHORUS
Too handsome (*He's too handsome*)
I've committed the crime / Of being ~~fit~~ sublime
Too handsome (*He's too handsome*)
I've broken the law / With the line of my jaw
Now I'm under arrest / For looking ~~cool~~ my best
I guess I'm just too handsome

Note - for video
Me looking into a mirror
Backing vocals sung by reflection?